Shaggy Dog Stories

Tales of the Countryside

Charles Parkes

Joe Cowley
best wishes
Charlie Parkes

First published in the UK in 1996, extended, and revised in 2023. The characters and events portrayed in this book are fictitious. Any similarity to real persons, living or dead, is coincidental and not intended by the author.

ISBN: 9798372797734
Imprint: Independently published

Cover design by: Art Painter
Library of Congress Control Number: 2018675309
Printed in the United States of America

To Elizabeth, my Life Partner, children and especially our grandchildren, Charlotte and William, who bring so much joy, song, dance and laughter to our lives. In addition, to you, the readers of this book, who have been so good as to take an interest in my flight of fantasy.

I hope you enjoy the book.

"Indulge your imagination in every possible flight."
JANE AUSTEN - PRIDE AND PREJUDICE

Contents

Preface

I published Shaggy Dog Stories in 1996 selling over 10,000 copies. With only two copies left on my shelf, I decided it was time to republish and search my brain for some new material.

My brain and I have been together for over 70 years achieving some remarkable things and some dismal failures! Measure once - cut once – buy another worktop, for example! These days I do find it harder to deal with irrelevant data. All I need is the bottom line. If I want more data, I will ask for it or Google it, or just switch off from my loved ones. I can be forgetful and find it hard to recall things but that is normal and does not mean that I am losing my marbles. Indeed, I have a full tin on my bookshelf.

I know that my brain has filed huge amounts of data unconsciously and it just takes a bit longer tracking it down. It is all in there somewhere! However, it is difficult to find what you do not know the brain has stored for a rainy day. Suddenly, something pops into my consciousness and I wonder, "Where did that come from? What triggered that thought? And why?"

As manager of Swanwick Men's Shed, I have observed various forms of Alzheimer's and dementia at close hand and fear the onset of these debilitating conditions in my old age. It is terribly sad to see skilled woodworkers unable to recognise the tools and machinery they once used to create masterpieces in wood. I have also seen how people have regained the ability to enjoy life as a member of the shed. For some it has been a lifesaver. For a bereaved member the shed becomes their family.

To offset dementia I keep The Times General Knowledge

crossword books dotted round the house to dip in to, as and when. It is a comfort to find that my brain function improves with practice but I also find them rather soporific. I also find that instinctively shooting clay pigeons on a fast and furious simulated day proves that my brain, eye and body can still co-ordinate. My motto is "Still shooting. Still living."

Over many years, I have written books on countryside law and conservation. Getting every comma and full stop correct in a legal text is pretty tedious and tiresome stuff. In 1996, I wrote a small book of Shaggy Dog Stories that was purely fictional and imaginative and great fun to do, relishing the freedom to write without constriction. The title and some of the tales hark back to stories told by my father from his army days, and I enjoyed embellishing them with detail based upon characters I developed from friends and family. I truly enjoy visualising a location or a character and describing them with a picture in words.

Imagination gives you the freedom to create your own characters and personalities. They are the actors in your theatre bringing your words, actions and locations to life to entertain an audience. In your imagination, you can do anything thought to be impossible. The story line can take over all my waking thoughts and I jot down notes, wherever I am, and rush home to type them up. Never let an idea get away as you may not find it again. Imagination can take you wherever you want in the world at any time in history, or the future, even to places that do not exist. I find the mental process invigorating and exciting and realise that the old brain is not dead or dying!

Being creative has been a hugely enjoyable, fun and rewarding experience leaving the brain energised as if it was on fire. Creative writing is a great exercise for the brain - all you need is a spark. As Jane Austen said, "Indulge your imagination in every possible flight." [Pride and Prejudice.] You do not need to publish just try short stories or your life story. No need for them to be fiction either, just write about what you know or have done.

In 2004 I took my wife on a railway holiday on the West Highland Line and Hogwarts Express. On the bleak and rain swept misty Rannoch Moor I saw a young woman leave the train and disappear into the mist. I began to imagine what might befall her, alone in the boggy wilderness. I told my "sister" Carla and fifteen years later found a spark of an idea that fired the imagination for a romantic mystery novel about The Hidden Glen in the Scottish Highlands. It is published in her name on Amazon as an EBook and paperback.

Rudyard Kipling, the author, not the cake-maker said,

"I keep six honest serving-men

(They taught me all I knew);

their names are What and Why and When and How and Where and Who.

Choose a person, a location or situation and apply the 5Ws and you are up and running. The data is all in that brain of yours somewhere.

The Pet Salmon

Some poachers will tell you that it is the excitement of sneaking a salmon from under the bailiff's nose, rather than financial gain, which drives them out in all weathers and at all hours. Consequently, the keen, astute bailiff and the furtive, expert poacher often become entangled in a never-ending battle of wits. This is the story of one such battle.

As dawn broke through the mist over the Hampshire Avon, Philip White peered from a hiding place he had constructed among the brambles and hawthorns some fifty yards from the water's edge. Three hours earlier, he had seen a light in Foxy's cottage. The door had opened to let the skinny, pointed, silhouette of his archenemy, Foxy Fern; slither into the night carrying what appeared to be a bucket.

The bucket had aroused Phil's curiosity. As a bailiff of many years standing, he thought he knew all the poacher's tricks and methods, but a bucket had never been part of them. He had run over the fields and settled in his hideout to await Foxy's arrival at the Duke's Pool. Phil passed the time thinking of the many occasions he had just missed catching Foxy in the act, and the times they had exchanged greetings on the riverbank. Foxy always had that “I know you know what I've been up to glint” in his eye. Perhaps this was to be Phil's day.

A rattling pebble on the stone-strewn bank woke Phil from his daydream. The morning breeze rolled away the mist to reveal the unmistakable shape of Foxy's body, the bucket at his side. Phil watched and listened hoping to get the evidence he needed. There was a splashing, ringing sound as if a fish was thrashing about in a half-filled bucket of water.

At last, Phil had caught him with a live fish. He had come across Foxy several times with a dead one, only to be met with such excuses as:

"I just found this one floating down the river Mr White. Looks diseased to me." Or;

"You've had poachers Mr White, I couldn't sleep so I went for a walk and found three of the blighters hiding this in the bushes. Is there a reward?"

Phil, unable to contain his excitement, ran to Foxy's side who appeared most unperturbed at being caught red-handed.

"Got you this time Foxy!" Phil proclaimed in a triumphant but rather breathless West Country brogue.

"Got me. How do you mean Mr White?" replied Foxy in his quizzical, cheeky way.

"Caught you with a live salmon, that's what I mean. It's the Magistrate for you this time!” crowed Phil.

"But this is my pet salmon. I can't be had up for a pet salmon!" Foxy bleated indignantly.

Previously, Phil had lost cases in court through some lame, half-baked excuse concocted by the poacher. The thought of Foxy evading conviction sent a shiver through him as his joyful revenge was momentarily arrested.

"Your pet salmon is it Foxy? You'll be laughed out of court with that one. No-one has a salmon for a pet!" retorted Phil, his air of confidence tinged with doubt.

"It's true Mr White," declared Foxy detecting the faintest glimmer of light at the end of an escape tunnel.

"Isn't it Sammy?" he added for good measure and effect, looking to the gasping, floundering fish in the bucket for confirmation.

Phil was dumbfounded. After all, he had seen him leave home with the bucket. It had to be one of Foxy's wiles. Nevertheless, what if it wasn't? Foxy was a big fish and not yet ready to be reeled in to Phil's landing net.

"And what do you and your pet salmon do?" asked Phil giving his fish some line.

"I keep Sammy in the bath and once a week I bring him down to the river for a swim. After about twenty minutes I give a whistle and he comes back." Foxy stated in a casual, matter of fact tone of voice. The light in the tunnel grew brighter.

"Can't you see that Sammy's all excited - he was just about to dive in when you came thundering up!" He added accusingly.

Phil roared with laughter and the more he laughed the more the doubt in his mind diminished. He picked up the gauntlet thrown down by Foxy.

"Let's see Sammy go for a swim then. Let's see you whistle him back." Phil challenged, thinking what a good yarn this would make at the next meeting of the fly-dresser's guild.

Foxy lifted Sammy into the water and after a momentary pause to establish his bearings Sammy gave a flick of his tail and glided into the river. Phil checked his watch. Foxy leaned back against an old tree trunk, his hands behind his head in a nonchalant manner. Neither spoke throughout the twenty minutes, although Phil managed the occasional "Pet salmon indeed!" in a tense chuckle under his breath, whilst glancing riverward for a glimpse of an approaching fin.

"Time's up Foxy. Let's see you whistle your pet salmon!"

"Salmon Mr White! **What salmon?"**

A Bird in the Hand

When the pheasant season draws to a close, a keeper can afford only a few moments to reflect on his or her success before making preparations for the next season. The keeper starts by trapping up wild birds, incubating the eggs, rearing the young, and later, releasing the poults to pens in the woods. There then follows a daily round of feeding and watering.

As the poults mature and wander into the surrounding fields, the keeper will dog them back away from neighbouring land and public footpaths. Nights will be spent patrolling the copses in search of predators on two and four legs, especially the vixen looking for a meal to feed her cubs. In addition game crops and woodland need to planted and managed, fences mended, bridges repaired and the shooting ground prepared.

Whilst in captivity the birds belong to the captor, but when released they become, in law at least, 'ferae naturae', wild and ownerless. The keeper's employer may spend many thousands of pounds on this unpredictable venture by way of wages, housing, equipment, feed and vehicles to ensure a plentiful supply of birds. Having made such an investment, it is hardly surprising that keeper and shoot captain will regard the birds as their own property, in captivity or otherwise. If not by law, then by natural justice surely, or "per industriam" – by one's labours.

One day a gamekeeper was observing a motorist on the road next to a copse who appeared to swerve at a cock pheasant strutting about in front of the car. Was it an accident or a deliberate attempt to poach it?

The gamekeeper hurried to the scene where the driver was about to place the dead bird in his boot.

An argument then developed over the driver's actions but there was insufficient evidence to establish his intentions. The keeper followed another tack by claiming ownership of the bird. Faint heart never won fat pheasant but the motorist stood his ground, claiming it was wild and that he had as much right to it as the keeper.

Neither gave ground as the keeper proffered reasons for ownership of the bird and then the motorist-come-poacher turned the tables.

“Well if the bird belongs to you then it is your responsibility to pay for the damage to my car!" he remonstrated pointing to the scratches on his nearside wing.

"Have you got a game licence?" You need a game licence to take or kill pheasants you know." replied the keeper, quickly changing the subject.

The motorist seemed totally flummoxed and the keeper seized the moment and the pheasant. "You'll be hearing from my solicitor about this!” raged the motorist.

"Aye well don't forget that lawyers and woodcock both have long bills!" advised the keeper triumphantly.

Finders Keepers

PC Wilson pressed hard on the pedals, his head down and back bent, as he strained to reach the top of the hill. The heavy 26" frame, police-issue, cycle, in regulation green was equipped with a capacious saddle bag to carry a plethora of administrative forms and other items essential for the efficient execution of his duties. Such items included fish 'n' chips, the occasional pheasant or his plumbing tools for the odd bit of service to the community.

His beat was wide and varied, ranging from an out-at-elbow council estate, to the well-heeled suburbs of Stubbing Court. Gazza's huge frame, cloaked in blue serge, relaxed as he freewheeled towards the enclave of grand houses occupied by local businessmen and his Superintendent! Spying a kestrel hovering over nearby stubble, Gazza alighted and, gazing skyward, removed his helmet to wipe the beads of glistening sweat from his brow.

"Hoy! You!"

His moment of tranquillity shattered, Gazza turned to find himself at the end of a long drive meandering through the immaculately kept grounds of Moss Cottage.

"Hoy! You there! Constable!"

A slightly rotund figure elegantly dressed in white silk blouse, tweed skirt, blue wellies and gardening gloves, waved her trowel at PC Wilson. The ever-astute Gazza, sensing his services were required, parked his cycle against the wall and strode purposefully up the drive.

"What are you going to do about that?" demanded the lady, her trowel pointing across the lawn. Gazza's eyes focused on a dark steaming mound of fresh dog poo, standing prominently on the manicured green sward. It was essential that his NVC's (Non Verbal Communications) did not leak the wrong message. But one of the qualities of an experienced officer is the ability to choose the right approach for every incident.

"Have you got a polythene bag Madam?" he enquired calmly. The lady disappeared to the potting shed returning with the aforesaid item. Taking the trowel from her hand Gazza tiptoed delicately across the lawn, trying to disturb the blades of grass as little as possible. Having pooper-scooped the offending pile he handed the bag to the lady and set off down the drive, his boots scrunching loudly on the gravel.

"What am I supposed to do with this?" she cried, holding the bag at arm's length.

"Oh if nobody claims it in three months, it's yours to keep Madam!" responded PC Wilson, his step quickening towards his cycle. His escape was complete as he mounted the bike and pedalled off as fast as his weary legs would allow.

Half a mile further on his radio crackled, "PC Wilson report to Superintendent Moss immediately! ! !"

"Oh well. Finders keepers....losers weepers." reflected Gazza.

The East Wind Doth Blow

Charles Sallis was a wise old man having graduated through the University of Life and two World Wars; he was now three years past his allotted time of three score years and ten.

Born and bred on the eastern edge of Norfolk he resided, where he was raised, in a cottage on a smallholding looking out to the marshes and the cold North Sea. He was well schooled in making a living from the land and the sea, sufficient to feed his wife Sarah, and three daughters, and put a little aside, but he was not a rich man by any means.

His services as a water diviner were often called into use when a new well was to be dug and he was able to turn his hand to repairs, plumbing and decorating. Everything considered he was a valued member of the small community.

His orchard produced large quantities of cider apples that he kept for cider-making. Cookers and eaters were either stored or taken to market with his other fruits. Market days were often intoxicating affairs but his faithful pony knew the way home with Charles sleeping it off in the cart behind. When not tending his vegetables and orchard, he would be in the marshes with his shotgun, sitting in a ditch waiting for wildfowl flighting in at dusk. The odd goose was enough to grace his table and feed the family but he also employed an 8-bore punt gun for his commercial ventures. Geese and duck would settle in large flocks on the sea, and he would lie in the punt quietly paddling as close as possible without disturbing the birds. One shot could capture a bagful for his regular customers.

Eels, sold alive, or better still smoked, brought in a pretty penny so early mornings were spent digging lobworms and threading them on to worsted yarn. A bunch of worms, or bob, was then suspended on a line from a large cork float. An eel's teeth tangle or catch in the worsted so no hook is needed, and it can be hoisted out of the water and flicked off into a tub or the bottom of the boat. He was adept with rod and line and netting mullet in the tidal rivers

He was an expert with nets being able to make and repair them. When the night was right, he would silently set a long net, held up with short sticks, in front of a warren while the rabbits fed on nearby crops. When startled the rabbits scurried for their burrows only to be entangled in the slack net.

Sailing so close to the wind he often had to think and act quickly if the farmer, or worse, the gamekeeper appeared on the scene. In those days the rights to take ground game were reserved for the Squire and the tenant farmer could only stand and observe rabbit and hare eating his crops. The farmer may have thanked him for a brace of bunnies and the protection of his crops, and be prepared to accept a pheasant for his silence. The Squire and landowner was no great friend to either and would soon have them in court if he could. The keeper was not open to such bribery and would do his utmost to carry out his duties to the letter. He also had a family to feed.

However, Charles did fall foul of the law occasionally and became conversant with defending himself in front of the magistrate, often a friend of the Squire. The local Police Sergeant, who prosecuted his cases, was not inclined to press the charges too fiercely, as he also had a taste for game. Charles often escaped with a small fine but felt indignant at prosecution for taking a wild bounty, free for the use of any man, as stated in the Bible.

One morning he rose and opened the curtains to see his beloved smallholding flattened, his vegetables crushed and bruised, fruit stripped from the trees and his fence broken down in several places. The adjoining field was owned and grazed by the Squire but on this morning, his herd of boisterous and mischievous young bullocks was nowhere to be seen.

Charles salvaged the damaged vegetables separating them into human consumption, chickenfeed and pigswill, before setting off for the Manor to remonstrate with the Squire. En route, he encountered the gamekeeper, Augustus Fozdyke, who met him pleasantly with a vague smile permeating his face. Charles knew he knew but Fozdyke stated he had been out chasing poachers all night around the fen and saw nothing of any rampaging bullocks.

Charles continued to the Manor where the offending bullocks, were contained in a yard. The Squire would have none of his allegations or demands for compensation for trespass and damage to his fencing and crops, even though Charles had seen them in the field the night before. Charles shouted at the stockman for confirmation but under the steely eye of the Squire, he shook his head and shrugged his shoulders. Faced with a wall of silence, Charles set off for home with indignance and rage festering inside him.

That afternoon he set off for the offices of Fry and Smallheap, Solicitors, Market Street, Holt. The long-established firm was located in a small narrow building, its traditional brick and flint ground floor topped by a Tudor style black and white timbered second floor. Charles parked his bike outside and entered the quiet front office reeking of floor polish and ancient papers. Miss Parsons, the secretary, looked him up and down through her half-lens spectacles; her grey hair tied in a bun on top of her head, greeted him with suspicion. He persuaded Miss Parsons that he had a great need to see Mr Fry on a matter most urgent. Her initial reluctance soon gave way when Charles mentioned the Squire and he was instructed to,

"Wait there! I will see if one of the partners will see you at such short notice." He was not offered a chair but took one just the same as he was as entitled as any man to be treated with civility.

"Mr Fry will see you now. Go to the top of the stairs. Knock and wait for Mr Fry to call you in."

Charles complied and soon received the call to enter. Mr Fry sat behind his gargantuan oak desk, the green leather top strewn with papers and files. An empty teacup and saucer lay to his right, and a cigar gently smouldering in a glass ashtray to his left. Mr Fry gestured for Charles to take the chair in front of the desk.

"Now what is this about the Squire, Mr Sallis?"

"Well before we gets down to business Mr Fry I am not a wealthy man so what will your advice cost me?"

"I normally give fifteen minutes free and thereafter I charge by the quarter hour. Let me give you some advice gratis to start, 'Nothing is certain in law except the expense.' The clock is ticking so give me a brief idea of your case."

Charles had rehearsed his complaint while cycling to Holt. He explained the location of his smallholding and fence adjoining the Squire's field. On retiring to bed, he saw the bullocks, about twenty in number, in the field. The next morning he rose to find the fence broken down and his vegetable plots flattened and decimated.

Mr Fry interjected, "I advise you again that law is expensive. Why not stand a quart and settle."

Charles explained his attempt to speak to the Squire who dismissed all his claims and sent him packing.

"Mr Fry I want him prosecuting."

Mr Fry sat back in his mahogany and green leather Captain's chair, swivelling a little to the left and then right as he mulled over his response.

"My dear Mr Sallis. You have suffered a wrong but it is not a felony, nor a misdemeanour, and you cannot prosecute the Squire for trespass. That is a civil matter."

"But the Squire has signs all over his land and woods that trespassers will be prosecuted!"

"Mr Sallis. They are meaningless and in legal circles we call them 'wooden falsehoods' aimed at keeping ne'er do wells, poachers and the like off private land." Mr Sallis had fixed Charles with a stare as he emphasised "poachers" making him feel uneasy.

"But that's not fair....." blurted Charles

"What's law isn't always fair Mr Sallis, but if you are intent on going to law then you must sue the Squire for damages at Common Law, seeking compensation for the damage to your fence, loss of crops, the inconvenience of travelling to my offices and my bill. We are now at the end of your gratis advice. Do you wish to proceed to law?" asked Mr Fry giving an indication of the length of his bill.

"Could you not lend me a copy of this Common Law so I can read it and defend myself?"

Mr Sallis you are not the defender. You are the prosecutor or in civil law the Plaintiff and the Squire is the defendant or Respondent. I cannot lend you the text of the Common Law for it does not exist."

Charles was befuddled and was about to speak when Mr Fry raised a hand to silence him.

The Common Law is not an Act of Parliament. It is part of English law derived from custom when man first lived in communities and by common sense agreed what was right and what was wrong."

"Like the ten commandments," interrupted Charles, "Thou shalt not steal...."

"Exactly right, Mr Sallis."

"So does the Common Law say cattle cannot trespass?"

"As I said, it is not written down and the courts must apply common sense to a situation. The first recorded writ for cattle trespass was during the reign of King John. Was it right or was it a wrong, known as a tort. The trespass was not your fault so you are justified in seeking compensation **IF** you can prove your case."

A further thirty minutes were clocked up on Mr Fry's watch by which time he had advised Charles to take out an information with the Clerk to the Court who would issue a summons and for Charles to present his case in person, simply, calmly and fairly. Handing Charles a note of his bill he wished him luck in his suit adding,

“If you fail then perhaps your bill could be settled in kind, Mr Sallis, as I am sure you have access to the odd goose or pheasant, although I am quite partial to a brace, **or two,** of roast partridge.” Charles nodded his understanding.

As he left for the door Mr Fry added,

“Oh address all your evidence and answers to questions directly to the Judge.” Charles nodded.

Charles took the advice and a few days later strode up the drive to the Squire’s house. Fozdyke was there to greet him and barred his way to the front door.

“What’s your business here, Sallis?”

“I am here on court business and I have papers for the Squire.” Proclaimed Charles, waving the summons under Fozdyke’s nose.

Fozdyke, taken aback by this approach, stepped aside to let him pass.

Charles heard the bell clanging in the hallway behind the heavy oak-panelled front door. Then the echoing tip tap of footsteps and he was greeted by the maid looking down on him from the top step.

“Tradesmen round the back.” She sneered and tried to close the door, which came to an abrupt halt against Charles’ hobnail boot.

“This is court business as I have a summons for trespass for the Squire.”

“What is all this commotion?” bellowed the Squire from his office just off the hallway.

The maid ran in to explain.

“What!” roared the Squire? “Summons? Trespass?”

The Squire, now enraged, emerged like one of his rampaging bulls, red-faced, bulgy-eyed and snorting.

Charles was now rather apprehensive and fearing what may happen next but he remembered Mr Fry's advice to remain calm and civil.

"I am here to serve this summons on you claiming compensation for the damage caused by your trespassing cattle." He said proffering the papers and pushing them deliberately into the Squire's hand.

"Trespass! Trespass! I'll give you bloody trespass! Fozdyke show this peasant how we deal with trespassers!"

Fozdyke jumped into action and Charles now feared a sound beating as Fozdyke had always wanted to get his own recompense for Charles' poaching activities. Fozdyke spun Charles around, took hold of his collar with one hand and his trouser belt with the other and frogmarched him on tiptoes down the drive giving him a resounding push on to the public footpath.

Mr Fry had advised that the Squire would not accept the summons gracefully and to make a written note of words and actions. Charles completed the certificate of service on the rear of the summons and duly returned it to the Clerk.

"See you in court Mr Sallis. 10am Monday 25th instant. Don't be late." He advised.

The day could not come soon enough and Charles was there by nine thirty. Fozdyke and the Stockman arrived together and they sat in the waiting room glowering and laughing at Sallis. The Squire arrived, and with him, a portly gentleman wearing a Barrister's wig and black gown, carrying papers tied with pink ribbon. The Squire pointed to Charles,

"That's him Trumpleton. That's the ne'er do well, scruffy, oik who wants to take me to law."

Trumpleton smiled and nodded his acknowledgement of Charles.

"Nigel Fortescue-Drake." Called the court usher. "Charles Sallis."

The Squire and Trumpleton brushed past Charles marching

briskly into the courtroom, taking a seat at the front of the court as indicated by the Clerk. Fozdyke and the stockman sat in the row behind.

"All rise." Called the Usher.

The District Judge strode to his seat, weighing up the participants before him. He nodded to the Clerk who confirmed the identities and addresses of Sallis and the Squire.

The District Judge looked sternly at Trumpleton, who leapt to his feet,

"Judge, I am Trevor Trumpleton, Barrister of Trumpleton and Snotgrove, Holborn Chambers, London. I am here to defend this suit against Mr Fortescue-Drake."

"This is a simple case of a claim for compensation caused by the trespass of a herd of young bullocks belonging to Squire Fortescue-Drake onto a smallholding owned by Charles Sallis. Mr Trumpleton, you are aware that I have read the papers pertaining to this matter?"

"Yes Judge I am."

"And yet your client is still prepared to contest the matter?"

"That is correct."

"Do you wish to take any further instructions from your client and advise him as to the possible outcomes, especially if he were to lose his case?"

Trumpleton looked at the Squire who shook his head."

"No Judge. Mr Fortescue-Drake believes he has no case to answer."

"Hmmmm. So be it. Mr Sallis your evidence please.""

Charles gave his evidence that he saw the bullocks in the field and next morning they were gone leaving a trail of destruction behind them. He estimated a fair cost for the damage to the fence, his crops and his legal costs. He also explained his attempt to settle out of court with the Squire.

"That stockman knows the truth of the matter but the Squire will not let him speak it."

Pointing at Fozdyke, he continued,

"When I was serving the court papers, that Gamekeeper, Augustus Fozdyke manhandled and frogmarched me down the drive...a man of 73 years." Charles demonstrated how Fozdyke had taken hold of his collar and belt with two hands.

"And then Judge, for good measure he booted me up the backside on to the public highway!"

The Judge made notes as the stockman and Fozdyke hung their guilt-ridden faces from his view. Fortescue-Drake and Trumpleton averted their gaze away from the Judge who was obviously displeased with their actions.

"Thank you Mr Sallis. **Most succinctly put**. Please wait there as I am sure Mr Trumpleton will wish to ask you **a few** questions. He has a train to catch back to London so I am sure he will not wish to **waste time** in court!" The Judge emphasising "a few" and "waste time" whilst fixing his eye on Trumpleton.

Trumpleton rose to his feet like an Admiral on the verge of winning a great naval battle.

"Mr Sallis. Can I confirm that you did not see a single bullock in your garden?"

"Yes, but......"

Trumpleton cut him short.

"Thank you Mr Sallis. Is it not true Mr Sallis that the weather in these parts is renowned, even notorious, for strong blustery squalls?"

"It is Judge, yes. It comes off that North Sea over the foreshore remarkably strong so it does. The land is flat you see."

Buoyed by Charles' helpful response Trumpleton continued,

"Is it true Mr Sallis that these notorious blustery squalls can tear up trees, bushes and wreak great havoc hereabouts?"

"That's true they do. In fact last winter I had an old oak tree come crashing down....."

"Thank you Mr Sallis." Interjected Trumpleton triumphantly now in full sail with the wind behind him and ready to sink his opponent with a final salvo.

"So how can you say then that it was the cattle that caused the damage and not these strong winds that you have witnessed?"

The Judge studied Charles looking for his response. Charles paused. Fozdyke and the stockman nudged each other smirking and Trumpleton smiled at the Squire who nodded his approval.

"Coz I ain't never seen the wind leave cow pats behind sir."

Forgive Not Their Trespasses

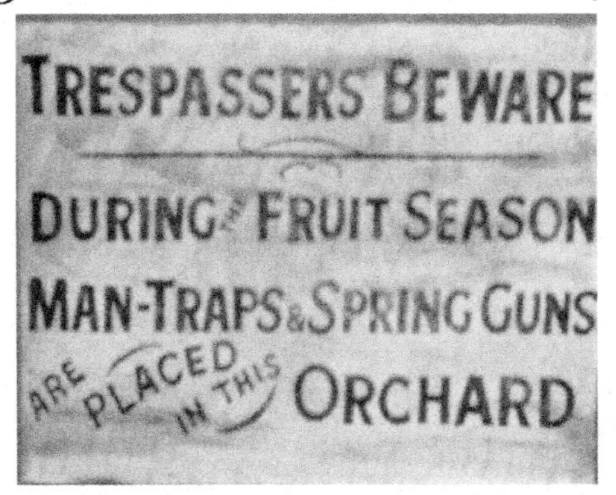

In 1901 Nicholas Everitt, a Norfolk solicitor, published Shots from a Lawyer's Gun, a humourous yet authoritative book on country law. His advice when dealing with trespassers was to witness them commit damage and then prosecute. To aid their guilt he suggested the loosening of nails on a stile or cutting through a plank across a ditch for the unwitting trespasser to demolish or fall through. Why not dig a pit, loosely covered with fragile material? If the trespasser should complain too vociferously and refuse to leave your ground to the nearest highway, then he can be knocked down, even bound hand and foot and carried off. No rights to roam in the early 1900s.

It was common practice to set mantraps, a terrifying and indiscriminate machine to catch the unwary. Alarm guns were also set triggered by a trip wire and firing a blank cartridge to sound the alarm to the nightwatchers.

His book tells the tale of one landowner who displayed a mantrap on a tree in front of his farm. Hanging from the fearsome jaws was a booted and trousered human leg severed at the thigh! This caused great consternation in the locality but no-one could identify a one-legged poacher limping round the village. Neither did they link the landowner with his friend, a surgeon at the hospital who had removed the leg in an operation.

Setting mantraps was made unlawful by Section 31 Offences Against the Person Act of 1861

"Setting spring guns, &c., with intent to inflict grievous bodily harm.

Whosoever shall set or place, or cause to be set or placed, any spring gun, man trap, or other engine calculated to destroy human life or inflict grievous bodily harm, with the intent that the same or whereby the same may destroy or inflict grievous bodily harm upon a trespasser or other person coming in contact therewith, shall be guilty of a misdemeanor, and being convicted thereof shall be liable to be kept in penal servitude."

However it remained lawful to set a mantrap in a dwelling-house - "Provided also, that nothing in this section shall be deemed to make it unlawful to set or place, or cause to be set or placed, or to be continued set or placed, from sunset to sunrise, any spring gun, man trap, or other engine which shall be set or placed, or caused or continued to be set or placed, in a dwelling house, for the protection thereof."

My father told me a true story of a man who had two incomes and was able to live on one and save his wage packets from the other. These were stored in a tin trunk in his bedroom. At some stage he realised his wage packets were disappearing so he set a trap inside the box. Sure enough he returned home to find a trail of blood on the stairs leading to the trunk.

The trap consisted of a steel pipe containing a shotgun cartridge, rigged to a tripping device and a firing pin. The police followed the trail of blood to a nearby house, up the stairs to find the neighbour dying in bed with a stomach wound. In spite of the most conclusive evidence of his guilt he denied the offence to his death.

The Complete Stalker

The hero of this tale had undergone a lifetime's apprenticeship in shooting sports but the pleasures of wildfowling and game shooting had begun to fade. He had to face the ultimate test of his field craft. A man alone in pursuit of the wild deer. Little did he realise however that it would take even greater cunning and craft to acquire the tools of his trade.

His bank balance was severely dented by the purchase of a quality rifle, albeit second-hand and this was only the start. Over the winter months, he took part in several B.A.S.C. road shows and seized the opportunity to acquire further pieces of equipment. He was renowned for his bargaining skills and at the end of the evening convinced one trader that it would be to his advantage to part cheaply with a gun cabinet rather than take it back to his premises. Arriving home in the early hours we silently manoeuvred the cabinet into his study where it was secreted until the opportunity arose to explain its presence - like a new dress.

"Oh that old thing - I've had it months darling!"

Not all this intrigue was apparent to me until the next road show when having pinned on his B.A.S.C. discount name badge; he disappeared into the stands and returned with a leather rifle sling. For the rest of the roadshow and the journey home he was pre-occupied with twisting, bending and flexing the said item. Being a stranger to rifles and stalking I assumed this manipulation was to make it supple and be a comfortable fit on the shoulder. I believe that in the antique trade the practice of distressing is used to make something appear older than it is. With antiques, however, the aim is to enhance, rather than reduce its second-hand value.

Boots, Loden cape, hat, and a DIY bi-pod almost completed the outfit. One last item was required. The venue was the C.L.A. Game Fair at Stratfield Saye. He arrived early on the first day, visited the stand, deposited his belongings and pinned on his B.A.S.C. discount badge. The stand was within knife-throwing distance of Malcberry's and the temptation proved too great. Within minutes he was the proud owner of a new hunting knife.

"I'll tell her it was only £15."

When stalking, the snapping of a twig, the faintest scent or the slightest movement will arouse the suspicions of the deer and send it scurrying away with never a shot being fired. In this case it was to be something far less subtle that was to cost him dear. He had left the VISA slip for the knife in the ashtray of his wife's car. His final acquisition was a new and expensive pair of lady's shoes!

THE MACHO RIFLE SLING
THE RAMBO KNIFE
Paley

The Shoot Dinner

It had been an icy finger-numbing December day at Boltby Park, as the shooting party returned to the host's house for a warming dram, clean dry clothes and the prospect of an excellent dinner, Pinkie, being renowned for his cuisine and hospitality.

The guns settled back in their armchairs, glass in hand, savouring the glow of the log fire and the aroma from the kitchen. Talk was of great shots and misses of the day, high pheasants, fast partridges and gun dogs. The dinner gong called them to the stately mahogany table laid with white linen, silver cutlery and cut glass. Conversation continued unabated but most managed a glancing survey in anticipation of the feast to come. Eyes were drawn first to a large central floral decoration, then the bottles of Margaux, and finally to the dishes of small, biscuit coloured balls, that aroused only temporary curiosity. They seemed vaguely familiar, were they an hors d'oeuvre or a savoury nibble?

The butler ceremoniously wheeled in a voluminous steaming tureen. Mouths watered in anticipation as the soup was ladled into their dishes. All served; they were ready to start, but something was amiss. Not a bread roll in sight! Perhaps an oversight. Would it be impolite to ask?

"Is anyone going to try the croutons?" invited Pinkie dropping a handful of the balls into his soup. The mystery was resolved. As croutons go, they were rather strange looking yet somehow familiar. Most diners followed Pinkie's example, tentatively sampling the soup-laden balls. Nods of approval led to further forages to the crouton dishes accompanied by the occasional "Must be wholemeal." Or "These are different - new line at Fortnum and Mason Pinkie?"

As soup and crouton levels dropped conversation returned to the day's sport while the butler served roast beef and vegetables.

"Oh by the way the dogs have all been fed for you," informed Pinkie. Several members responded with appreciative remarks and were about to plunge knives and forks plate-wards when Pinkie continued,

"They enjoyed the croutons as well!"

The awful truth had dawned. Pinkie, a renowned practical joker, had fed his guests on Chudleigh's Chunks. The guests swallowed heavily trying to prevent the croutons from reappearing unceremoniously on the table as Pinkie rocked with laughter.

"You should see your faces!" he exclaimed triumphantly and burst into another bout of laughter. A smile crept across one or two faces as the initial revulsion disappeared.

"I'd better tell the wife to have a bucket of water ready in the bedroom." quipped one.

"Yes and don't go near any lamp posts on the way home." Jibed another, as the table erupted.

The moral of this **true** story is "beware any host renowned for practical joking."

The Boundary Dispute

God looked out across the Gardens of Heaven where the dew-drenched foliage sparkled like crystal chandeliers in the emergent sun. He breathed in the aroma of the fresh moist earth and the perfume of sweetly scented flowers as the birds sang their joy at the dawn of a new day.

Lifting his eyes to the horizon, He could see the distant red glow and wisps of smoke emitted from the Fires of Hell. His heart was sad and heavy as He thought of those lost souls whose life on earth had committed them to an afterlife of torment. A far-off group of figures caught his eye. In Indian file, the four men stumbled wearily along the path from Hell, arms hanging Iimp at their sides, bodies fatigued by their night of un-heavenly exertions.

As the party of shoot captains progressed slowly, homeward God's anger subsided and His kind heart forgave their transgressions, after all there would always be humans unable to resist Old Nick's temptations. God also felt partly to blame as he had a joint responsibility to maintain the fence twixt Heaven and Hell.

God set off towards the night revellers. All but one hung his head in guilt and shame in the presence of the Almighty.

This one pot-bellied, bleary-eyed individual drew heavily on a cigarette. A bought of heavy coughing, brought a red flush to his face and removed, temporarily, the cheeky impudent smile of satisfaction.

God spoke.

"You were warned that cigarettes would bring your life to a premature end. It seems that you have continued your earthly excesses in the life eternal. Remember Mr Beale that I only allowed you past the Gates of Heaven because you were a salmon fisherman."

Beale, adopting his most humble, Uriah-Heap-like posture, responded,

"Yes Sir, I know, and I would like to add that there is absolutely no truth in the false and malicious rumour that I fished the worm and not the fly."

Heartened by this good news God continued towards Hell. Beale gave a sigh of relief and led his party home.

Arriving at the boundary, God's worst fears were confirmed as the fence was holed in several places.

"I wondered how long it would be before you turned up." hissed the sulphurous voice of God's oldest adversary. Erecting the fence was a joint exercise to prevent lost souls from cutting short their expiation, and the saved souls from succumbing to temptation. Even the greatest enemies have to come to certain understandings and there had been a gentlemen's agreement to repair the fence in turn.

"I believe it is your turn to carry out repairs." God replied.

"I don't see why I should. It's all your people causing the damage, coming down to my place every night trying to get the best of both afterworlds." Mocked the devil.

"Regardless of the cause it is your turn." God argued.

"I had it repaired last month." Retorted the Devil angrily.

The argument continued until God declared that the police should be called to resolve the matter. To ensure fair play, each party agreed to send for an officer from his own side of the fence. Sergeant Titterton duly arrived from Heaven and Superintendent Mason from Hell. The officers listened patiently to both parties, consulted together and declared that boundary disputes were a civil matter.

"I suppose we will have to put this in the hands of a lawyer." Declared the devil.

"And where will I find a lawyer?" muttered God.

The Sybarite's Tale

8 across Sybarite [9]. Thank heavens for Google and the Ipad when it comes to The Times on Saturday Jumbo General Knowledge crossword - my Saturday morning indulgence with coffee in the summerhouse.

A Sybarite turns out to be a person who is self-indulgent in their fondness for sensuous luxury with antonyms of: hedonist, sensualist, libertine, pleasure seeker, playboy, epicurean, glutton, gourmand, gastronome, bon vivant, bon viveur, connoisseur and epicurean.

The name originates from 720BC and the city of Subaris an ancient Greek city in south-eastern Italy noted for the luxurious, pleasure-seeking habits of many of its inhabitants.

The answer was "voluptuary." I like voluptuary, it seems to flow off the tongue and can be used with great expression to describe our character perfectly as one seeking gratification of sensual appetites.

But, what has all this to do with bull fighting you ask? Nothing at all, except it reminded me of the tale of one such sybarite and voluptuary who felt the need to escape from the Costa del Sol and its trendy fashionable beach clubs, populated by celebrities and beautiful people. Andalucía had more to offer by way of food, culture and the experience of the real Spain and its people.

A hire car took him to a small hotel in Seville close to the Plaza de Toros de Sevilla, the largest and most important arena for bullfighting in Spain. The 18th century oval arena located in the El Arenal harbour district, can accommodate 13,000 spectators and has a unique Baroque façade, dating from 1762-1881.

Our intrepid epicurean immersed himself in the local culture by attending the evening event leading to the coup de grace delivered by the Matador's sword, the Estoques de Torero.

Gentle reader I trust you appreciate the educational benefits of this tale but apologise if you know it all.

He had been advised to dine at one of the many tapas restaurants adjacent to the Plaza de Toros and found Ole Cojones de Toros, a quaint 18C establishment tucked away in a quiet side street behind a small red door. Inside his eyes grew accustomed to a dimly-lit portrayal of old Spain. Ancient maps, a black and white T.V, and mounted heads of bulls, were among some of the vintage mementos hung on the wall.

The waiter and owner took him to a table quickly establishing that his new diner was "Ingles" and introduced himself as "Manuel."

He immediately recognised the questioning look in the eyes of the Ingles and clarified,

"Non senor, I am not from Barcelona." [The fictional character from the BBC sitcom Fawlty Towers.]

The Sybarite smiled and nodded his understanding and explained his desire to sample the delicacies of the area.

"Si senor the signature dish of the Ole Cojones de Toros is a rare delicacy to be found in the name, Cojones de Toros." Seeing the quizzical look on the Sybarite's face he continued,

"Senor we take the Cojones, the testicles of the bull that died in the bullfight this evening. They are sliced and sautéed in red wine and tomato sauce with wild herbs from the mountains and served on a bed of rice."

"Manuel that sounds fantastic. I will have Cojones de Toros."

"Senor, would you like wine with your Cojones?"

"Oh yes Manuel. A bottle of your best **Ree-oh-ja** please." Pointing at the wine list.

"Senor may I recommend a local wine grown on my brother's vineyard in the Province of Aldi. It is called **"Ree-okk-a"** and tourists find it goes very well with **"Lass-agg-ni"** and Cojones."

Our Sybarite relished every mouthful as he relived the brave battle of the bull against overwhelming odds and the inevitable demise he had witnessed that evening. Truly a dish to die for. Unless you are a bull of course!

He enjoyed the meal so much he ordered the same for next day. The meal was again delicious.

"Senor did you enjoy your meal and Riocha?"

"Manuel they were even more delicious, but they were much smaller than the ones you served yesterday."

Manuel nodded whilst shrugging his shoulders and replied,

"Si, Senor....... but sometimes the bull......he **WINS!**"

Eli and the Whale

Gentle Reader please read this story with a broad Dudley accent.

It was Sunday. The late morning sun shone brightly through a chink in the curtains at 27 Gasworks Lane, Dudley. A shaft of dust laden light fell on Eli's sleeping face causing him to stir and wake. His legs flopped to the floor as he sat up and perched on the edge of the bed. With head held in his hands, he regretted the previous night's excesses and cursed as his hand groped the bedside beer crate, only to find an empty Woodbine packet.

As the alcoholic mist cleared, his eyes focused on the fishing rod leaning in a dim corner of the room and Enoch's voice echoed around Eli's pickled brain,

"See you down the cut about eleven."

Eli dipped his right forefinger in a half-drunk cup of cold tea and cleaned his teeth, the cool liquid moistening and soothing his dry and swollen tongue. Brushing down his sleep-creased trousers and shirt, he shouldered his fishing basket, took up his rod and went downstairs. Opening the fridge door, he took a swig of milk from the bottle standing next to his maggot box, before stepping out on to the cobbled street.

Eli called at the corner shop for twenty Woodbines, a box of Swans and a paper. Cupping his hands to shield the flaring match Eli lit his breakfast and crossed to the worn steps leading down to the towpath. He could see Enoch in the distance, sitting with his back against the glue factory wall, basking in the warm sun, his cap pulled down over his eyes.

"Now then our Enoch - 'az yer caught owt?"

"Only a whale our Eli." Replied Enoch casually.

Eli looked at the keep net which appeared empty except for three bottles of beer cooling in the murky canal water.

"Didn't yer keep the whale then Enoch?" enquired Eli.

"No Eli. Didn't have any spokes in it!"

Spot Plays Dominoes

Spot the dog always accompanied his faithful master, Tom on his evening visits to the Mucky Duck. On this particular evening, Tom went to his usual seat by the window and tipped the dominoes out on the table. Spot sauntered over to the bar, ordered and paid for two pints of bitter and took them back to Tom's table. Spot jumped on the chair opposite Tom and one man and his dog began to play fives and threes.

All this activity had been observed, open-mouthed, by a couple of bed-and-breakfasters on a weekend break from the city. After watching several rubbers, curiosity overcame their shyness and they approached Tom, whose eyes never moved from the table as he sensed their hovering presence.

"That's a clever dog you've got there old chap." They enthused.

"How's that then?" Tom enquired dryly.

"We saw him buy the beer and then play you at dominoes!" squawked the townies wife.

"Well he isn'a that clever. He hasn'a wun a game yit tha knows!!!"

The Origin of Stonehenge

"We've only just go the scaffolding up!"

Pheasants and Polar Bears

Through the centuries, the ingenuity of the hunter and poacher has developed many devices and techniques for taking game, wild animals and fish. The hunter seeks to use sporting means but the poacher may resort to cruelty in search of a quick profit. For example, pheasants taken in rattraps, or choked on a raisin containing a stiff bristle, or a baited fishhook tied to a peg.

Whilst guns, nets and traps have always proved popular and productive, some of the more unusual practices include dropping a noose on a pole over the heads of roosting birds, stupefying them with burning sulphur under the tree, intoxicating them with grain steeped in alcohol, or setting a gamecock fitted with steel spurs to fight belligerent cock pheasants.

One has to admire the simplicity, and perhaps the audacity, of a Victorian poacher's trap made from nothing more than an empty champagne bottle. The double irony being that the bottle, and perhaps its contents, were acquired from His Lordship's cellar, thereby providing the poacher with the best in food and drink. The bottle was rammed neck down, into deep snow and the funnel shaped holes left to freeze. Once baited with peas, a pheasant was able to feed from the top but would eventually reach too far into the hole, lose its balance and fall in headfirst. It was then a simple task for the poacher to harvest his illegal crop by plucking the helpless birds from the traps, leaving no trace as they melted away in the morning.

It seems that such methods, ingenuity and inventiveness were not restricted to the English poacher. In fact, the champagne trap, like the Labrador retriever, may have its origins in countries far removed from our shores. An Eskimo folk legend describes a similar method for hunting polar bears. The Eskimo, like the Victorian poacher, made use of the most readily available materials, which ruled out champagne bottles. His only requirements were an ice-saw and bait. Apparently, polar bears, raiding explorer's camps, developed a taste for dried peas, regarding them as a great delicacy. No! This is not the story about feeding lions with fish, chimps and mushy bees! The records of the Hudson Bay Company actually show the import of dried peas in wooden barrels and traded for furs.

A party of three or four was necessary to deal with a fully-grown bear, and armed with peas, ice-saw and harpoons; they trekked into the frozen wastes. At a suitable spot, a hole was cut in the ice. Peas placed on a piece of wood, or dried sealskin, floated on the water in the hole and they laid a trail of peas to draw the bear to the trap. Now the polar bear is as wary as any pigeon and the Eskimos hid in a small igloo type hide for many hours until a bear approached the trap. As the bear leaned over for a pea, the Eskimos would emerge from the hide, run up to the bear and kick it in the ice hole! The legend does not give any information as to the success rate or the survival rate of the hunters.

The Fishing Party

"Time gentlemen please!" The landlady of the Manchester Arms threw the towels temporarily over the pumps and waited for the strangers to leave. Adjusting the shoulder strap of her bra for the umpteenth time that evening, she waddled round the shabby bar, with its threadbare green linoleum floor, and cream gloss walls now stained in shades of yellow and brown by years of tobacco smoke.

As she collected the empties, regulars stuck to their seats, waiting for some serious Saturday night drinking to start behind closed doors. One group of men, huddled head to head at a round table in one corner, cigarette smoke puthering from their midst like a smouldering volcano.

Jean's stubby fingernail-bitten hand, festooned with gold rings, descended into the crater to remove the pint glasses and their last dregs of Boddy's. Boddingtons bitter is brewed within sight and smell of Strangeways Prison tantalising its inmates with its frothy ferment, and most of these lads had seen the brewery from both sides of the wall.

"Our Jack's out the back. Go out through the kitchen." Whispered Jean, nodding over her shoulder to show the way. Their conversation interrupted, the heads turned towards Jean. One of them turned away again sharpish as his nose met her perspiring armpit and the wandering dirt-trimmed bra strap.

"I've got the freezer ready so don't come back without a bag full."

"Come on lads. Time to go." Said Broken Nose rising to his feet.

"Let's go and show them country wallies how to fish."

A peel of drunken laughter erupted from his cronies and they marched out, conga style, through the kitchen. In the backyard, Jean's husband was waiting in his battered Transit enveloped in clouds of blue smoke billowing from the noisy exhaust.

The fishermen sat uncomfortably on plastic beer crates amidst rods, tackle boxes, maggots and dustbin liners. Fortunately, one of them was a refuse collector on the local council. The van spluttered up the long hill out of Hyde, leaving behind the deep blue carpet of Manchester sparkling with streetlights as far as the eye could see. In front, beyond Mottram, rose the Dark Peak, the moors of the Peak District, now featureless in the night sky, save for distant hilltops silhouetted against the pale moonlight.

The van came to rest in a narrow country lane next to a public footpath.

"Here we are lads. Out you get. Quiet now, there's a farm just behind us."

Following Broken Nose's orders, the fishermen spewed forth from the van and stood quietly surveying their strange surroundings. Night owls they may have been in the city, but the deafening silence of the countryside, broken only by the barking of the farm dog, unnerved them.

Broken Nose led the way along the muddy footpath across the fields towards a wood, the moon disappearing behind the clouds as they entered the trees. Wing Nut, the youngest at seventeen, and so-called because of his sticky-out ears, ducked and weaved as a bat flew overhead. His oversize wellies caught a root bringing him and his tackle crashing to the ground, earning a stiff expletive-ridden rebuke from Broken Nose.

The trees opened out as the footpath continued alongside a drystone wall. Leaving the path the party clambered and scrabbled over the wall with the agility of arthritic gorillas, and they found themselves on the bank of a small, secluded reservoir rimmed by a low range of hills.

"Not far now." Broken Nose barked in a loud whisper. He called his troop to a halt at the waterside adjacent to a stone hut and a series of small fibreglass tanks fed by a stream from the hillside.

"Don't look like a good fishing 'ole to me!" exclaimed Eddy, supplier of the bin liners, whose fishing expertise amounted to hand lining for crabs off Blackpool pier.

"Look Eddy this is where they breed trout for them green-wellied lot. Them that pays an arm and a leg to fish in the rezzers. This is where they chuck pellets in to feed 'em. That's why it's a good spot and what's more we're fishing for rockall...!" retorted an exasperated Broken Nose.

"I've never heard of Rockall Trout." sniggered Wing Nut.

Ignoring Wing Nut's ill-timed attempt at humour, Broken Nose issued the order to get set up along the bush-lined bank, and there they sat as if it was a Sunday morning on the canal. Over the next hour thirty or forty tame trout, tempted by a host of golden wriggling maggots thrown around the floats, received the last rites and fell into one of Eddie's bin bags.

Only the distant drone of heavy lorries on the trans-Pennine Woodhead Pass broke the silence as each man concentrated on his bobbing float. A light twinkled briefly in the bailiff's cottage high on the hill as Broken Nose drew heavily on a roll-up, reflecting on the days of his youth when equipped with a plastic carrier bag, cheese sarnies, Mars bar, a water-filled lemonade bottle and a packet of five Park Drive ciggies, he set off on the bus to explore this valley. Having been sent packing by some officious person at the dinghy club for messing about near the boats and cursed by a green-wadered fly-fisher for disturbing the fish with his stone skimming he had given the country up as a bad job.

Wing Nut appeared at his side.

"Can I fish with you? It's no good where I am." Pleaded the spotty youth, trying to hide his fear of the dark.

"Push off! Try further up! There's no room here!" Snarled Broken Nose.

Wing Nut sloped off, his wellies, being two sizes too big, slapping against his calves.

Broken Nose's attention was drawn to his submerged float and quivering rod as another trout fell to the maggot. The bushes rustled behind him.

"I've told you once you wally - fish further up. There's no room here!" he growled anticipating Wing Nut's return. A shiver ran down his neck as something cold and hard pressed against his ear.

"If you want to find a wally in the country - bring one with you." Said a voice, philosophically in a quiet country accent. Broken Nose spun round on his beer crate to find himself staring into the barrels of the bailiff's twelve bore.

Mr Henderson's Runaway Coffin

Mother was extremely proud when I followed in father's footsteps to become a Police Constable, and she immediately started knitting a balaclava in dark uniform blue for those cold winter nights. The non-police-issue item was stashed away until my transfer to the Peak District where much time would be spent rescuing motorists stranded on the Snake Pass. In 1956, my father had the same experience rescuing motorists and recovering the body of one poor soul who did not make it. So mother knew best.

After my initial training at Pannal Ash, near Harrogate I was pleased to be posted in the small market town of Ashbourne. It was near home, I had fantastic digs [lodgings] with an old retired couple. George, a pipe smoker, retired from the highways department but the ticking pendulum clock on the wall was always set twenty minutes fast to get him to work on time. George had a dry wit and after watching me devour a large chop with veg and two portions of apple pie would say,

"I bet tharz not had none no worse." His wife would give him a clout with a tea towel, "Oh! You!!!!!"

They were like grandparents and all at £4.50 per week bed and board.

My beat attachment with a seasoned officer revealed we did not arrest or prosecute many people. There was little to do, apart from the occasional RTA [road traffic accident, now known as RTC – collision], a sudden death, a rare crime to record, but we never recorded theft of cattle or sheep as livestock had a tendency to "stray" and not be stolen! To record them as a crime meant paperwork and never-ending questions about the state of one's investigations.

Four weeks of riding in a Moggy 1000 [Morris 1000] Panda car later, and I was let loose on the unsuspecting public, patrolling the town centre on foot. I suppose it was re-assuring for the good residents to see a uniform presence on their streets, but for me foot patrol was mundane and I wandered from one tea spot to another, in the back of a shop or even a swift half in a public house. The market place chippy was good for a sit down at the end of hours helping myself to pie and chips. A large brown enamel teapot sat on the gas ring simmering a brew of "builder's tea" complete with milk. I avoided it like the plague!

I think we had our first telly in 1955 and I recall father stringing a long piece of wire round the lounge trying to get a signal for the black and white TV. I do not recall any soaps at that time but Dixon of Dock Green was the nearest thing to East Enders. Jack Warner was the epitome of the friendly local copper, who knew everyone including all the villains. All very tame, and then along came Z Cars zooming up and down the East Lancs Road around Liverpool. With its northern edge, it injected a new element of harsh, gritty realism into the image of the police and, after 801 episodes, the program and the characters were spun into a separate series called Softly Softly.

Perhaps it was all too softly, softly as evidenced by the Thames TV programme, The Sweeney tackling armed robbery and violent crime in London. Starring, John Thaw as Detective Inspector Jack Regan and Dennis Waterman as his partner, Detective Sergeant George Carter of The Flying Squad, screeching around the docklands at high speed dealing with a seedy and violent underclass that the public had never encountered.

Life on Mars began in 2006 telling the story of a Manchester police officer who mysteriously finds himself working as a police officer in 1970s Manchester. Life on Mars, and its sequel, Ashes to Ashes, combined mystery, supernatural, science fiction, time travel and police procedural drama genres. The storyline took some following and I am not sure I quite fully fathomed it, but travelling back in time to the seventies conjured up many memories. Date stamp a policewoman's knickers? While she was wearing them? Never happened! Honest Guv!

I suppose there was a bit of Regan and Carter in most Bobbies and I recall one officer using Reagan's term, "Back to the factory" and Gene Hunt's, "Fire up the Quattro." But there was no chance of any such action at Ashbourne, a point reinforced when I returned to the District Training Centre for two weeks "continuation training." We were no longer "Sprogs", probationer constables. We were nearly at the end of our two-year probation and about to be proclaimed fully-fledged Constables. By way of introduction, the instructor went round the class asking for examples of incidents we had experienced. I was among lads and lasses from the northern cities, Nottingham, Leeds, Manchester, Liverpool and Sheffield. I was aghast at what they had been through. I rarely left the town centre foot patrol and was only allowed to drive the Panda to deliver it to the earlies sergeant to use the next day. I used to drive very slowly to pass as much time as possible. I recall one idle officer taking me to an RTA and saying we would not bother with the breathalyser procedure as it took a lot of time and trouble.

I had to think quickly of something to offer from my experience. Two things sprang to mind. There had been a case of cattle maiming where cows had been seriously injured and the cowshed set on fire. Being a country cop in the midst of city cops often attracts comments about one's relationship with wellingtons and sheep! The ace up my sleeve was the recording and monitoring of aliens under the Aliens Act 1905. In those days, anyone coming from a foreign country was classed as an alien, and on arrival at their destination, required to report to the local police. A report to Special Branch, in carbon paper triplicate, was required for Swiss persons attached to the local Nestle factory and sounded quite important.

Pounding the beat was monotonous, but I was able to socialise with many of the young ladies. Father had warned me about entanglements with the opposite sex that might result in marriage. It was the age of miniskirts and leather boots proving far too much for a hot-blooded young copper. Father was right and fifty years later, I am still entangled with the love of my life. A significant number of brownie points were gained when said wife proofread this part,

"Ooh. That's nice." She said. [More points than I got for attending her choir concert on the evening England lost to France in the Qatar World Cup!]

On my rest days I returned home to "have my bottle filled" by Mother competing with the landlady to feed me better, wash and iron my uniform etc. We had blue cotton collarless shirts with a stud fastening that left a green mark just below your Adam's apple. It meant you could wear a shirt for more than one day if you were not a sweaty individual. I dreaded the question about what I had been up to the previous week, meaning what exciting police work had I been engaged in. There was never anything interesting to report and I do not think she meant evenings in my yellow Ford Anglia or Mini-van with a young lady.

City cops had an easy life to some extent. They were always double-crewed and assistance was always close at hand if they got in trouble. All they had to do was shout on their VHF car or UHF personal radios. Crimes would be dealt with by CID and RTA's by the Traffic Department. I was the other extreme working 1700-0100 plodding the town centre going from point to point. A point was a designated telephone box where you attended at the given hour and waited for ten minutes in case the Sergeant or Inspector came for a booking. The points located around the town ensured coverage of the beat. I had no radio. I was expected to deal with whatever came along. The town was part of a large Rural Beat covered by the Panda car but on many occasions, I was a lone officer, on foot covering two such areas. If I got in trouble assistance was twenty miles away if I was lucky.

The chippy closed late evening and the pubs cleared by 1045pm, leaving a few stragglers on the marketplace, so the town was dead. I often passed time with a friendly gang of bikers who met there. They were no trouble, all were in work and bikes were their hobby. Around midnight I grew concerned at the presence of two local miscreants. One was a huge slob of a youth famed for being drunk and was often found sleeping in the town toilets. He was from the adjoining town. The other was a local youth renowned for his readiness to fight anyone and being a "bit handy."

For some reason these two had decided not to like each other that night and were now shaping up for a fight in the middle of the street. There was a lot of pushing and shoving and exchanging threats. I knew that the previous week officers had tried to arrest the giant slob who offered passive resistance by spreading himself across the single door to the Moggy 1000. Normal practice would have been to transport him to the adjoining beat or over the Hanging Bridge in to Staffordshire. I also knew the other lad was "a bit of a handful."

Gradually they pushed each other off the street and across the pavement and were now up against the Post Office window. Reflections from the street lamp told me the pane was flexing under the pressure and, if it broke, I would be forced into action. The bikers were at hand and, with great wit and ingenuity, I instructed,

"Get these two off the street before that window goes in."

My newly deputised posse of "double 0 licensed to kill agents" leapt into action forming a scrum to squeeze them up the narrow confines of Town Hall Yard. Problem solved. Community policing at its best.

The phone in the call box started to ring instructing me to attend a sudden death across the town, the home of Mr Henderson, a widower. His morning milk was on the doorstep and the

Derby Evening Telegraph hung out of his letterbox, alarming his neighbours. He was found in bed and the doctor had certified death but was unable to issue a certificate for the cause. My job was to examine the scene and the body for signs of suicide or violence. Occasionally we had to gain entry via a ladder and bedroom window, or break a pane with my truncheon, but thankfully, a neighbour met me at the door and provided most of the details for my report to the Coroner.

The undertaker arrived in a black van containing an equally black coffin-shaped tin box with a loose lid. It was customary out of hours for undertakers to arrive unaided seeking the assistance of the bobby to help remove the body. Sometimes this was no easy task especially in this case; a narrow, corkscrew staircase accessed the upper floor of this small terrace. The tin box would not go round the corners so a zip-up body bag was laid at Mr Henderson's side and we placed him therein.

With a loop handle at each end we were able to slide the bag round the helter-skelter stairs and place the deceased in the box waiting in the hall below. "Burke and Hare" snatched the body into the van and the job was done for the night. Mr Henderson was stored at the chapel of rest ready for the mortuary next day.

I was back on duty at 0900 reporting to the sergeant about the sudden death but not about the incident on the marketplace. I completed my report and set off to the mortuary at the local hospital to meet the undertaker at 10am, hand over Mr Henderson and identify him to the mortuary staff. Morticians could be a strange breed but not surprising given their daily task. They had their own sense of humour and tricks for the young bobby,

"Want a cuppa lad?" they would ask.

"Get the milk out of the fridge then."

No sooner had I walked out of the police station than the Sergeant's office window opened barking instructions to go to an RTA on the Market Place. Patting the leather wallet containing all my procedural forms I set off hotfoot along Church Street before turning onto the cobbled market place. It was more of a triangle than a square with a steep hill along one side climbing out of the town centre towards Buxton. The top half beyond the market became steeper still and was a notorious hot spot for brake failures on heavy lorries hauling stone for the quarries. A descending lorry had missed a gear and the brakes faded. Luckily, it came to rest in the front of a black van travelling uphill and the road was completely blocked.

The impact had twisted the body of the van springing the rear doors open thereby spilling its contents on to the hill and jettisoning Mr Henderson's tin box on to the road, careering down the hill, screeching and scraping on the tarmac. Slithering through the red light on the pedestrian crossing, it came to rest with a great thud against the front door of Boots the Chemist, flinging the lid into the air, to the great consternation of passing shoppers.

On hearing, the commotion a sales lady screamed,

"Oh my goodness it's Mr Henderson." recognising a long-term client. The pharmacist ran over and said,

"What does he want?"

"Have you got anything to stop me coffin?"

Most of this tale has a semblance of autobiographical truth and it is true that I told Mother the tale about Mr Henderson's runaway coffin, but Mother, like a fat brown trout in Duffer's Fortnight had swallowed the Yellow Drake mayfly, hook, line and sinker, and was heading for the landing net.

Spot and the Hat

Tom and Spot were walking through town one market day when a gust of wind caught the hat on a gentleman a few yards ahead of them. Spot, mistaking the brown Harris Tweed for a large rat seized upon it and shook it until well and truly dead. The gentleman was not amused and turned upon Tom.

"I say old man your dog has torn my hat. What are you going to do about it?"

"Can't say as I'm going to do anything about it." Responded Tom, reassuring Spot with a pat on the head.

"He were only acting natral. Any road up! Wot duz tha expect wearin' one o'them rattin' 'ats?"

"I don't think I like your attitude!" the gentleman snapped.

"Tweren't my 'at he chewed! It were your 'at he chewed." retorted Tom

Carry On Fishing

Two overnight trips to Cumbria resulted in no more than a glimpse of flashing silver salmon and some impromptu swimming practice in chest-waders.... just testing the Falkus Theory of Feet First Flotation. With clothes and appetite whetted by the River Eden, it was with great excitement that I accepted the invitation for a few days on the River Orchy at Dalmally with John and Steve. My experiences on that trip will be of benefit to anyone planning a similar expedition - there are several points you may not have considered...........

I had set up with fly and spinning rods but a trip to Walkers of Trowell was necessary to replace the devons, and tobies left clinging to the bottom of the stony Eden. I would also need worming hooks, weights and swivels in good numbers, plus flies to suit the river.

One evening we met to tabletop all our equipment and sort out the menu and shopping list. This was a self-catering affair and one should not underestimate the eating power of three gannets fishing in the fresh air for up to twelve hours a day. The evening ended with John and me watching a video on the art of Spey casting. From the comfort of fireside chairs, we waved our arms in the air, but sadly, our actions were more akin to a demented orchestra conductor than the fluid style and grace of Hugh Falkus.

Confucius said, "The man who cuts logs for the fire is warmed twice." When it comes to worm gathering, this is not a philosophy my friends subscribe to! Not for them the backbreaking slog with a spade. Following a friendly farmer's plough is a useful and leisurely way of employing one's children at fifty pence a bucket. In Scotland many years ago, when enquiring about the availability of the garden fly, I was informed,

"Worrums! Worrums! The worrums are scurcer than the fush." A statement, which proved to be true when three acres of fresh earth provided a mere couple of pints of wriggling bait.

There is no Sunday fishing for salmon in Scotland, so the day was spent travelling north to our riverside chalet. That evening I realised that if one was not able to choose one's fishing partners one must be prepared for a certain amount of culture shock. After all a man who can eat, a large raw onion in white vinegar and a pot of salt for his tea, followed by three pints of “heavy” [bitter beer] must have an amazing constitution.

With only a few days to find and catch the elusive salmon we needed to make the most of our time, so all daylight hours would be devoted to fishing. We retired early, only to be rudely wakened at 6am by a prolonged fit of coughing from the toilet. It seemed that the onion and cigarettes and 'heavy' were wreaking havoc at both ends of Steve's body.

Fishing early is not difficult if one is sufficiently motivated. Within an hour, the breakfast pots had been washed and put away. Not a fact to be made available to one's loved ones at home. With the Range Rover loaded with flasks of coffee, cake, clothes and tackle, three hopeful fishermen set off up the Orchy. On those rare occasions when all the right conditions of water, light, running fish, temperature, choice of fly etcetera come together, the salmon is still an elusive individual, with its mind set on one thing. Think back to the days of your youth; what would have tempted you away from the promise of a night's pleasure with a piece of hot stuff? Consequently, we were rather dismayed to find a river showing its bare bones in an area having one of the highest rainfalls in the country.

Steve jiggled a worm along the stony depths of Black Duncan. John and I chose a wide, shallow stretch to practice the Spey cast. Within half an hour, the line was singing through the rings as hand and eye regained their co-ordination. One lost fly, one broken hook and one parr was the result of three hours hard fishing. We met to discuss tactics over coffee and cake. A note for wives here, that one eight-inch fruitcake will be consumed by three men at each of these meetings. It is not a delicate operation requiring cake knives and doilies - just ripping into three pieces with one's bare hands.

There were many fish in evidence appearing restless and frustrated, like ourselves, at the lack of water. Steve and I moved up river from Black Duncan and worked a deep narrow channel under a far bank with worm and fly.

At the shout of "Fish on!" I abandoned my rod and went to Steve's assistance with the landing net. At his insistence, I took the rod and played the fish to a chorus of instructions and abuse from the bank. To say I was thrilled is an understatement. However, the catch was down to Steve and I would have to wait for the satisfaction of hooking one for myself.

It was at this time that I met Jimmy, the proprietor's man, clad in well-worn tweed Plus Fours and deerstalker. A wise and wizened old Scotsman, he kept an eye on guests, fishing any vacant beats at his leisure. His encouragement, advice, eternal optimism and peculiar logic became a source of enlightenment and amusement, especially his tales of his days as a ghillie and stalker on highland estates.

Dalmally has one small shop and a mobile butcher who passes through once a week. Take your own or plan ahead. Jimmy acquired a haggis on my behalf and I asked him about cooking the wee timorous beastie.

"Och well. You boil it in a pan."

"For how long Jimmy?" There was a pause,

"Och, a wee while." It was obvious who did the cooking at Jimmy's and I thought it pointless to continue the conversation.

We returned to the cabin at midday for breakfast. There was to be no respite - one cooked whilst the other two fished in the pool below. I wondered if we would be so keen as the days progressed, but then I remembered the words of John Buchan;

"The charm of fishing is that it is the pursuit of what is elusive but attainable, a perpetual series of occasions for hope. Any hour may bring to the most humble practitioner the capture of the monster of his dreams. But, with hope goes regret, and the more ardent the expectations of the fisherman, the bitterer will be the sense of loss when achievement fails him by the breadth of the finest hair. It is a bitterness which is commonly soon forgotten, for the same chance may occur tomorrow or next week."

A new day dawned to the sound of the early morning smoker's cough and, when breath allowed, a string of expletives extolling the pleasures of the weed. For one whose bodily functions grind to a halt away from home it was most enlightening to find a man who needed to go three times a day. Such a fact may seem extraneous until you realise that when nature calls chest-waders can prove to be a rather obstructive form of apparel, especially when the shoulder straps are underneath fishing vests, jumpers and jackets. Most difficult to get down in a hurry.

On an isolated riverbank, the only public convenience is the open countryside, and including a wad of your favourite soft tissue will prove to be a great comfort. One may develop a preference; some might even call it a fetish, for fresh, damp moss as a substitute. Four words of warning. Ensure that hooks and flies left in coat pockets are not allowed to come in contact with your unused toilet tissue. Secondly, beware of exposing bare flesh in stalking country where the irresponsible shot may mistake your bare bottom for the back end of a deer. Thirdly, if any member of your party happens to be a practical joker, beware deposits in the immediate proximity of any tackle left on the bank. Fourthly, make sure you are the one that hands out the cake.

Do not believe that by including a first aid kit, one will be considered to be overcautious or a wimp. It has to be remembered that doctors and chemists are few and far between in remote areas and that time lost for treatment is lost fishing time. My wife, a nurse, had provided for all eventualities and whilst unpacking I was subject to a good ribbing as my ice cream container spilled its pills and potions across the kitchen.

However, he who has the last laugh laughs longest. It was rewarding to see the relief on Steve's face as he discovered the comforting warmth of my haemorrhoid cream. One morning John woke to a thumb throbbing in two places. I took great delight in lancing the offending lumps with a sterilised number six worming hook and the application of an antiseptic spray. Burn cream also soothed his fingers singed whilst testing to see which hot plate was on!

The river consisted of upper and lower beats to be fished on alternate days. Tuesday was blank and Wednesday saw Steve and I back at Black Duncan. I fished the channel where Monday's fish was hooked. After a couple of hours, Steve joined me and we both tried the channel with worm. Fish had shown in two spots and having just reeled in, one rose in front of me. I cast a couple of yards above the ripples, as if dropping a fly in front of a feeding trout. The line bowed in the current, I could not feel a fish so pulled hard on the line. There was a lot of slack and nothing happened. Then I felt a slight wobble and hopes started to rise. On pulling hard again the line tightened, the rod bent and the fish set off upstream, turned and charged downstream leaping and standing on its tail.

The emotion of the moment blanks out all those books and articles on playing salmon. I could hear Steve's voice but it seemed that I was in a microcosm. With all thoughts centred on the fish, I remember hoping that the knots would hold as it ran up and down the river, stripping line from the reel. As the fish tired, I backed slowly across the pool towards the shallow pebbled shore where Steve tailed the catch safely inland.

I fished with less urgency for the rest of my stay and took time to watch the buzzards and golden eagles soaring high in the glen and chat with Jimmy. We came across Jimmy one morning fishing at Black Duncan. His tackle had to be seen to be believed. The rod was a combination of materials lashed together from several rods. No doubt, he could catch fish with it in places that Hardy and Orvis would fail in the hands of lesser mortals. It reminded me of a story in the local paper many years ago, about a monster trout caught in a burn by a juvenile holidaymaker. Locals and visitors alike had failed to catch the legendary fish on all manner of flies and baits. This young man took it with a cold chip.

Jimmy's logic confused us all again,

"Aye well it's no right to catch a salmon today at all. I wuddna come out me sel!" Why was he fishing?

The water continued to fall along with our expectations of further fish. Jimmy appeared at one of our morning coffee, cake and hip flask sessions. His timing was uncanny. The answer to our problems was a prawn. We had none. But, we soon knew a man that had some. Jimmy slipped a packet of prawns surreptitiously from the back of his hand into Steve's pocket. You would have thought he was a drug dealer or a spy on a secret mission.

One salmon was to be my tally for the four days but I did see Steve take three fish in half an hour from the same spot. He also achieved a lifelong ambition of "catching a salmon with a fag on." How do they manage to light-up under water?

Was it really worth it? I could have bought smoked salmon from Sainsbury's for £12 per pound. My single fish provided the most expensive buffet on record at around £70 per pound. With my prize frozen and tucked up in a sleeping bag, I set off for home. A brief stop at Tyndrum's souvenir shop reminded me that other people did exist on the planet. I had not seen many in the last few days, no radio, no television, no telephones. Was it really worth it? Every penny!

Poetic Justice

Paul's line fell sweetly across the current carrying the fly over a tail of calm water. It fell into a large bow with the fly held firmly behind a rock, a renowned salmon lie. Heart pounding he gripped the rod until his knuckles glowed white, pulling in the slack until the line was taught and he could feel the knock of the salmon as it shook its head to free the hook. Unable to do so the fish ran upstream and downstream, leaping in the air for freedom and stripping the reel in an epic battle of man against fish.

As the fish lay before him, Paul surveyed his prize fleetingly as he reached for the priest to administer the last rites. Paul's hand wavered in the air, priest aloft in readiness to deal the mortal blow.

"Please don't kill me!" cried a faint gasping voice.

Paul's hand froze. Was that a voice or the cry of the circling buzzard? No! Imagination surely! His hand reached skyward once more –

"Please don't kill me!" The voice was even more desperate. Paul looked about him but there was nothing to be seen. Was it the cows tearing at the grass or a ghastly, ghostly voice sent to haunt him?

Paul focused on the inky blackness of the salmon's eye.

"Please don't kill me!" pleaded the voice.

Paul contemplated the impossible. Was it really the fish talking? Should he engage the fish in conversation? What does one say to a fish?

"Yes, it is me talking to you! The fish! Please put that priest down!"

The priest fell with a thud on the grass. Paul, looking around him to ensure no one was watching or listening, bent forward and whispered,

"Are you a talking salmon?"

"Yes, I am a talking salmon!" replied the salmon confidently and somewhat indignantly.

"Have you got a name?" enquired Paul attempting polite conversation.

"My friends call me Rusty. What is your name?" enquired the fish.

"P-P-Paul." was the stammered reply. "Am I classed as one of your friends?"

"Not if you're going to hit me with that priest!" retorted Rusty.

"I wouldn't dream of such a thing" replied Paul as he grabbed the priest and flung it into the depths of the pool.

"Look P-P-Paul, if you keep me out of water much longer you won't need the priest! Put me in the water to get my breath back and we can have a chat."

Paul returned Rusty to the icy current.

"That's better P-P-Paul." called Rusty.

"Are you English?" enquired Paul.

"Scottish actually." responded Rusty who continued, "I was spawned in this river five years ago and I have since travelled the oceans."

"I bet you have seen some sights." Paul enthused.

"Oh yes. Last year I swam round the wreck of the Titanic. Do you knowP-P-Paul. that the tables are still laid with plates and cutlery, all the furniture is in place, chandeliers, everything, just as those poor helpless passengers left them!"

Paul nodded open-mouthed as Rusty continued,

"I found it so moving that I wrote a poem which has just been published."

Paul was astounded. As a part-time writer himself, he knew the difficulties humans had in getting works into print, let alone a talking fish.

"What is your work to be called?"

"The Titanic Verses by Salmon Rusty."

The Sheep Dip

Newcomers to any occupation are always eager to demonstrate their ability and enthusiasm for their chosen career and this is particularly pronounced in young police officers fresh from the training school. Brimming with knowledge and confidence, they cannot wait to see some action and long for the day when they are free to walk the streets alone.

One such tyro, a PC Platt, was posted to a small town in the heart of the countryside, much removed from his hometown of Manchester. Compared with the television image of police work, walking the beat in a quiet market town was somewhat mundane. There were no big drug busts, no high speed chases around derelict docklands, no vice squads, no blaggings. Just the occasional septuagenarian kleptomaniac at the local supermarket, a drunken brawl when the single night-club turned out, a few parking tickets (for tourists only) sudden deaths, the occasional breathalyser and hours of traffic duty on hot Sunday afternoons as endless tourists fought for places in the overcrowded car parks. Whenever he met up with colleagues from the busy towns and cities, he had to suffer their jibes about sheep and wellingtons and "What's that funny smell."

Working out in the sticks does have some advantages however. The locals are very friendly and still hold the local bobby in high esteem, especially the young lasses who welcome any new blood with open arms.

Rural beats cover vast tracts of open land and the lone country officer needs to be self-reliant and able to deal with anything that comes along. He or she must be master or mistress of all trades. His efforts being rewarded with a sack of potatoes, free-range eggs, a rabbit or two, the odd pheasant, a spot of fishing, or a day beating on His Lordship's estate.

And so it was that one day the Rural Car Driver was on a training course and our young freshman was summoned to see Sergeant Hall.

"Here you are lad. Take this Form J and get off to Peak Top Farm. The sheep need dipping to prevent sheep scab and it's got to be done properly. Take your wellies. Are you sure you know what to do?"

He was not sure of the exact procedure to be followed but was more inclined to show the sergeant he knew what to do.

"Yes Sarge. I have to make sure the dip is the right strength and that the sheep are fully submerged." He had heard that much from his colleagues chatting in the canteen.

"Ay that's right lad. Just make sure they go right under though and that you don't miss any. Don't let them tight-fisted farmers put too much water in, and don't get that new uniform dirty either." He instructed.

Young Platt remembered looking at some old books in the Parade Room and found a small dog-eared paperback called WHAT TO DO and WHEN TO DO IT by FRED FOSTER (Ex-Detective Superintendent of Durham County Constabulary). Price 1/9 and published by the Police Review Publishing Company in 1946. This handy guide advised officers on such contagious diseases as Epizootic Lymphangitis, Glanders and Fowl Pest.

Turning to page 31 Platt found the entry for Sheep Scab Order, 1938 and the list of official forms he needed to serve and complete.

Armed with new knowledge, forms and wellies he savoured his newly won freedom as he drove through the country lanes high on the moor. The distant and isolated Peak Top Farm was situated a mile from the road along a rough gated track. As he approached the stone house and outbuildings, two collies ran out snapping at the wheels, jumping and snarling at his window.

It seemed an eternity before the Tyson brothers emerged from the dark foreboding portals of their cottage, to reassure him that the dogs were not dangerous. Opening the door a few inches he put a tentative foot on to the cobbles, both eyes firmly fixed on the two dogs lying in tail-twitching anticipation a few yards away. His sigh of relief was the signal for a rapturous canine welcome as the two dogs leapt playfully about him, their paws leaving muddy stripes all over his neatly pressed uniform.

With one hand protecting his most vital organs from the flailing feet, he proceeded towards the Tysons, trying to divert the animals' attention by deftly aimed flicks with his wad of official forms, which were soon in shreds, fluttering about the yard in the stiff moor land breeze.

The Tysons were an odd couple. As brothers and bachelors, they followed a lonely existence on the hill farm. The weekly mobile shop and postman were the only visitors. Apart from taking sheep to the market, they seldom ventured into town or anywhere else for that matter.

"What can we do for thee then bobby?" enquired Jethro, the eldest brother.

"I've come to do the sheep dip." He stammered nervously holding up the tattered remains of his forms.

"That Sergeant Hall sends us a young'un every year for the dipping. Dunt he Joseph?" Joseph nodded in agreement, as he gave the young'un a good looking over.

"There's an idle wind today." Shuddered Joseph, as he observed the grey clouds scudding across the horizon.

"An idle wind Mr Tyson? Does that affect the dipping?" enquired the intrepid Platt.

"Nay lad. An idle wind is a cold un. It goes through yer instead of round yer! Tha'd better 'ave sum tay fore tha starts. It's thosty wok and it'll warm thee. Get thee sen in bi fire." advised the kindly Jethro.

PC Platt ducked under the low stone lintel, his eyes straining to see from the light of the doorway and the glowing embers from the range. He sat in a large fireside chair, its arms and back threadbare from years of daily use. He felt uneasy as he caught Joseph's glare.

"That's Joseph's chair bobby. Sit thee sen over ere." Advised Jethro.

The uncomfortable young officer moved to the large wooden table, which filled the kitchen-come-living room. His eyes now accustomed to the dim light he became more aware of his surroundings. The table, like most of the furniture in the room, had become a final resting place for old newspapers, Farmers Weekly's, rusting tins of rat poison, hoof oil and other farming sundries with faded, peeling labels; gin traps, rabbit snares, shotgun cartridges and numerous cats. Propped in a corner by the door he could see a shotgun and a rifle, partly hidden by several crooks and sticks, and lengths of baling twine hanging from a nail above. There was a peculiar unique smell. A combination of sheep, cat and dog, paraffin from the oil lamps, years of dust, burning peat, and logs drying in a basket by the fire, musty newspaper, old wellingtons and who knows what else.

"What's this for?" enquired Platt picking up what appeared to be a pair of pliers with a small thick rubber band over the jaws.

"Them's for castrating lambs." Informed Joseph.

Platt remembered the occasion when Sergeant Hall had threatened him with a similar operation after an irate father had caught him in a compromising situation with his daughter.

Jethro filled a brown earthenware teapot from the blackened copper kettle hooked above the open fire. Platt was ready for a cuppa, to relieve the choking dryness brought on by his nerves and insecurity. Jethro noticed the amazed look on his face as he struggled to swallow the strange brew.

"It's evaporated milk, out o'tin. We've no milkman up here Bobby." Platt sank the first mouthful and sipped delicately at the remainder, slowly growing accustomed to the taste.

"Duz tha' tek tobacco young'un?" asked Joseph pulling a tin from his jacket pocket. The words were music to his ears.

"Thanks. I don't mind if I do Mr Tyson." Platt replied, who had been unsure whether to smoke or not in the strange surroundings. Joseph took a paper from the tin charging it with a carefully measured quantity of Golden Virginia. He looked up and stared at Platt as he licked the edge of the paper and rolled the cigarette in his stubby dirt-grained fingers. Platt would have preferred a hygienic mass produced ciggie, but a fag in need is a fag indeed, even though it turned out to be half a fag as Joseph tore the roll up in two for them to share.

"I think we had better get on with the job." Announced Platt in a more confident manner, anxious to finish his task and return to civilisation.

"Tin's there b'th door." Grunted Joseph pointing to a five gallon drum, "and dip's round back." Platt grabbed the drum, dashed for the sunlight and fresh air, and made his way to the sunken, water-filled trough. Two hundred and twenty nine bleating sheep waited reluctantly in a pen next to the dip. The brothers soon joined him.

"Go steady wi' that dip. It dunna grow on trees tha knows." Pleaded Joseph, as Platt poured a generous measure in to the trough.

"It's got to be the right strength, else the Ministry men will have you do it all again." Chided Platt, in a warily defiant manner. Joseph just shrugged his shoulders and muttered something unpleasant about officialdom and interfering bureaucrats.

The brothers grinned at each other as Platt slipped and slithered on the concrete ramp, wrestling with a wriggling, uncooperative ewe.

"Have yer dun this afore young'un?" enquired Jethro. Platt shook his head.

"I'll show thee." Said Jethro helpfully, opening the gate to let a ewe into the narrow corridor leading to the trough.

"She'll not go in easy." He advised, grabbing the stubborn animal by the scruff of the neck and the tail. In one fluid movement, the animal was launched headfirst into the murky disinfectant.

"Her head's to go under an all." He continued, whilst holding her down with a broom at the back of the neck.

"Thee have a go bobby. And mek sure they stay in furra whole minute, else Ministry men will mek thee do it all agin." instructed Joseph.

Platt entered the arena. Letting a sheep out of the pen was simple, but he failed to appreciate the strength of an animal unwilling to take its annual bath. Several sheep later, he had the hang of it. He relaxed and began to enjoy his labours as the brothers urged him on with encouraging words, mugs of tea and half roll-ups. Several hours dipping in the fresh air had brought a flush to his spotty complexion and he was relieved to see the last dripping ewe join the flock.

"Tha's dun a good job Bobby. Tha's no bad furra young'un. That Sergeant 'all knows 'ow ter send 'em." Jethro enthused. "Come on in and git thee sen weshed and cleant up." He continued, patting Platt on the back and guiding him toward the house.

"Let's see what our Joseph's got for thee." Platt lit up one of his own king size filters in anticipation of another one of Joseph's roll-ups.

After a cold wash in the stone sink, Platt was shown into the front room, which was spotlessly clean and tidy. A carpet square covered the bare boards, stained black between the carpet edge and the walls. The best room was a Victoriana collectors dream - with its polished mahogany sideboard, a china tea set in a display cabinet, the ancient phonograph, a pile of 78 records in dog-eared covers, brass and copperware, oil paintings and cut glass. PC Platt was a modern intrusion in a living museum of rural life. In the centre of the sideboard, between a pair of silver candlesticks and standing on a circle of lace, was a faded sepia photograph of a middle-aged woman, a rosary and crucifix draped around the frame.

She seemed vaguely familiar to young Platt...

"Would this be your mother Mr Tyson?" he enquired reverently, sensing her presence"

"Ay it is that Bobby. This is her room." Replied Jethro, his voice falling to a whisper.

As Platt gazed at the shrine, Joseph broke the silence...

"Git thee sen up tut table young'un and git stuck in."

Platt took his place and tucked into rabbit stew and vegetables spread out before him on best china and white linen. The main course, apple pie and wedge of cheese were all washed down with several glasses of homemade elderberry wine.

"Tha likes thee food and drink young'un." commented Joseph.

"Oh aye. I do that MrTyson. You're a good cook." complimented Platt.

Joseph's lips almost parted in a flicker of a smile.

"Tha'd best be on thee way now Bobby, else Sergeant will be after thee!" said Jethro rising from the table. Platt left the brothers, as he had first encountered them, leaning on the wall and set off down the track to the world he knew. The glow of satisfaction at a job well done was tempered by the state of his uniform stained beyond all recognition with muck and dip. What would Sergeant Hall say? The thought of a sound rollicking concentrated his mind and a short while later he pulled up outside his lodgings to change his tunic and trousers. As he climbed back in the car he noticed a box on the floor which he opened to reveal two bottles of elderberry wine and forty king size filter tips in his favourite brand.

His efforts had been appreciated and rewarded. All he had to do now was to make out a duplicate Form M Certificate of Dipping in the presence of a Constable. Platt marched proudly into the sergeant's office and presented his paperwork. Sergeant Hall stood warming his backside in front of the open fire.

Any problems with the dip then young'un?" he enquired.

"No Sarge. All dipped good and proper'" He announced. "Those Tyson brothers are a bit eccentric though Sarge. Do they come from an odd family?" he enquired.

"Aye the whole family is a bit strange. My missus is a Tyson you know." Responded the Sergeant looking up at a faded sepia photograph framed above the mantelpiece,

"That's her mother."

Addendum

The above tale did reflect reality in many cases and I am obliged to an officer recounting her experience when a farmer came in to Matlock Police Station to report his sheep had been worried.

"I was 19 & a Townie. Just couldn't understand him. Eventually I said "Just how worried are they?"

His reply, "They're dead Duck!"

Spot at the Station

In his days as a ghillie in the highlands of Scotland, Tom often met guests at the local railway station and brought them up to the big house. The station was no more than a platform serving the isolated rural hamlet. Tom sat on the platform bench and lit his pipe and Spot lay at his side. The train duly arrived and the stranger alighted rather warily, seemingly in the middle of nowhere.

"Excuse me. This is Glen Fardoon, isn't it?" he enquired of Tom.

"Oh arr, this be Glen Fardoon station all right, but it's a good hour's walk to the village." advised Tom.

"Don't you think it would have been more convenient to have the station near the village?" enquired the gent.

"Oh aye, we thought o' that but decided it were a better idea to have it next to the railway line!"

Terra incognita

Gentle reader, the story above harks back to the days when the railways opened up vast areas of Scotland for sporting pursuits, especially salmon fishing, stalking and grouse shooting. Station halts were no more than a platform in the middle of a desolate wilderness. Corrour on Rannoch Moor is a typical example still used today by tourists and walkers. In the 19C, as regards the sporting of the far north, Scotland was almost a terra incognita [not mapped or documented] There were no trains beyond Inverness, and to get there needed a journey to Aberdeen, and from there by the slowest of slow railways, followed by carriages and carts. Initially, there were no sleeper trains but by the mid-19th century, it was possible to take a more comfortable paddle steamer from London to Aberdeen.

As Scotland became more accessible, the well-to-do would ship their entire household, gamekeepers, dogs and servants for the season. The final lap of the long and slow journey to the sporting lodge involved carriages and carts, but one estate was only accessible by carriage to a loch and then steam launch to the accommodation.

William Alexander Adams was an early pioneer and his book, Twenty-Six Years Reminiscences of Scotch Grouse Moors details his expeditions to Dalnawillan just south of Thurso renting vast areas of moor for walked-up grouse over pointers. He employed a local keeper but took all his dogs and equipment, family and keeper from Warwickshire on the arduous trek to Dalnawillan. One interesting aspect of walked-up grouse is that the birds would pack-up in coveys and flushing early and out of gunshot so a hawk style kite was flown to keep the birds in cover until the pointer scented and marked them.

Adams bemoaned the transport links but still managed to shoot and fish across the northernmost and desolate part of Scotland, often staying a in a shepherd's croft. Eventually he built a five-bedroom lodge near to Altnabreac station, for the use of his family and shooting parties.

He says, "The railway was stuck down in the centre of the moorland to take its chance four miles from Dalnawillan Lodge, no road, or footpath even, in any direction."

Being the proprietor, Adams had no choice but to build four miles of road to the station for the comfort and convenience of family and guests.

However, the finest example of arriving in style, [probably pre WW1], was the Admiral of the Channel Fleet who "parked" his flotilla of warships in Duart Bay opposite Torosay Castle, Isle of Mull for a few days grouse shooting. A watercolour in the castle depicts the scene.

Spot and Patch

Every Friday night Spot would meet his friend Patch, the giraffe, outside the safari park and go for a drink in the village pub. Their attendance was something of an attraction and people would travel miles to witness the spectacle. Locally the Mucky Duck was nicknamed the Dog and Giraffe. At first, the two animals were more than happy to down the free pints bought by curious onlookers but the novelty eventually wore off and they tired of being in the public spotlight.

One Friday they decided to change venues and tried the ale at the Blue Cockatoo, an old coaching inn converted to a jazzy, colourful, brightly lit rendezvous where so-called popular music defeated any attempt at conversation. The trendy patrons, obviously accustomed to the unusual and bizarre, paid scant attention to Spot and Patch.

Spot bought the first round and engaged the bar maid in conversation,

“I came in this pub seven years ago.” He informed.

“Well I’m serving as fast as I can!” retorted the harassed barmaid.

Patch, being a once-a-weeker, soon found the ale going to his head, even though it did have a long way to go. A few pints later, his legs gave way into a four-way split and he lay helpless and immobile on the floor. Spot, unable to move his friend, headed for the door, only to be stopped in his tracks by two gorillas in monkey suits.

"Tha'd better not leave that lyin' there." Threatened a gorilla.

"That's not a lion. It's a giraffe." Responded Spot as he nipped through the bouncer's legs and into the street.

The Soul Fisherman

AJ's ambition was to catch his first salmon and with this aim in mind he took a beat on the Nith for two weeks. For six days, his line flailed the waters as he tried every type and size of fly without success. As the evening closed on the sixth day he sat exhausted and frustrated on the bank, glaring angrily at the flashes of silver in the pool below.

"I would give anything to take just one of you." He shouted in desperation.

"Did I hear you say you would give anything to catch a salmon?" enquired the sulphurous voice of the Devil appearing at his side. Lucifer was dressed for the occasion in tweed Plus Fours and a specially made deerstalker with holes to accommodate his horns.

"Yes anything. I've been here all week and not even had a fish look at my fly." The hapless soul replied.

"I know." responded Lucifer sympathetically, "Your case was brought to my attention three days ago and I have watched your lack of progress with great interest. It is within my power however, AJ," .....continued Lucifer, placing a comforting hand on AJ's shoulder.... "To change all that in return for a small remuneration on your part." He hissed.

Lucifer's sprat hooked the mackerel and AJ sold his soul! Over the following week, AJ had tremendous sport. Having caught his first salmon he went on to land a score of fresh-run fish. On the last day, he had a long and momentous battle with a thirty pounder. AJ sat by that same pool where he had met his benefactor and dropped dead with contentment.

Now in his short spell on earth AJ had been a decent sort of chap and one would have expected him to pass through the Gates of Heaven with little difficulty. However, a moment's weakness on the banks of the Nith and the lure of the salmon had landed him outside Hell's fiery furnaces, where Lucifer, now cloaked in black, waited to claim his forfeit.

Lucifer walked with AJ, past the fires of Hell until the tormented screams of worm fishermen, downstream nymphers and other lost souls, could no longer be heard. They came upon a superb stretch of salmon water. AJ was instructed to open a large parcel bearing his name, which to his pleasure and surprise contained a complete set of Hardy rods, lines, flies, reels and all their accessories.

AJ tackled up and with his first cast took a magnificent salmon. Casting again he hooked a second, and then a third. Throughout the day, his line sang out perfectly, cast after cast, no wind knots, no tangles, no lost flies, no hooked branches, and no hooked and lost fish. He had a fish with every cast. At the end of an exhausting day he enquired, "How long can I fish this truly enchanted beat?"

A quiet smile pervaded Lucifer's face,

"For ever, and ever, and ever."

Tug O'Rabbit

Over many years of talking to gamekeepers, I have heard many tales of things done and seen when night watching and lamping. A common question in gamekeeper circles is,

"Have you had many foxes lately?" referring to control by means of a lamp and rifle at night. For the keeper lamping is an expected part of his job-description and requires that after a hard day in the field tending his game, early morning dogging-in the straying birds away from his boundaries, feeding, and a whole host of tasks, he must turn out to scour the fields. He can often call upon neighbouring keepers or shoot helpers for company but lamping remains a solitary occupation in all weathers.

A good countryman needs to be proficient at field craft and seek imaginative ways of defeating "Charlie." [the fox]. One astute individual preferred the warmth and comfort of his bed to being bounced around on the back of a pick-up in search of his foe. Why not bring Charlie to his bed? His cottage bordered the fields, so he placed a fresh, rabbit carcase by his garden gate with a string tied to a leg. The other end was fed through his bedroom window and the bars of his brass bedstead. His trusty rifle was primed and ready at the side of the window and, placing a loop of string under the blankets and over his big toe, he would retire for the night. A tugging at his leg roused him from his slumbers and he would leap to the window and despatch the fox. Back to his slumbers.

One night, however, he was awoken rather abruptly and whatever was on the other end was pulling him out of bed! There were two foxes yanking on the carcase! Both despatched, but thereafter he rigged the line to some wire coat hangers trusting that the rattling bedstead would wake him.

It is amazing what one may encounter in the middle of the night in deepest, darkest countryside. Well you can imagine some of the goings-on but one lamper swung his lamp across the field to illuminate a man with a cat on his shoulder! When challenged he explained that he had two cats, one was missing and so he and the cat on his shoulder were searching for the lost pussy!

Prince's First Poachers

The nightclubs had spewed their drunken, noisy and troublesome contents onto the streets to be whisked homeward in a tangle of taxis. The town centre fell silent, allowing Inspector Thorpe and Sergeant Whyte to settle down to a sandwich and a frame of snooker. Neither were talented players but every frame was hotly contested.

"You'd think we were playing for the town hall clock!" The Inspector would exclaim, frustrated by the Sergeant's safety play. Neither fully knew the intricacies of the rules, which occasionally led to considerable argument. Inspector Thorpe sometimes had problems deciphering which ball had been struck or whether one had been hit at all. The fact that he once dived into a swimming pool with his spectacles on may explain a lot! On the other hand, he could spot a lost coin on the town streets when patrolling the beat, snatching it like the chameleon's ballistic tongue would take a fly.

He was the better player of the two and everything was hunky dory while he was winning. He was also the master of gamesmanship when the chips were down. His simple strategy was to disrupt his opponent's concentration by talking during a shot, denouncing good shots as flukes, bemoaning his own bad luck by proclaiming,

"I must have shot a bloody robin!"

His party piece, however, had to be experienced to be believed. Like all good snooker players, he was able to foresee the next shot and would plan to silently pass wind, adjacent to the cue ball. One can imagine the effect on Sergeant Whyte lining up his shot and dipping his nose into the invisible noxious cloud.

One such night everything had gone against Sergeant Whyte and the two parted in sullen silence following controversy over the rules of play. It was about 4am as dawn broke on a fine May morning and a stroll in the peace and solitude of the countryside would soothe the savage breast. Sergeant Whyte pulled up behind two of his patrolling officers.

"Get in here." He snapped. "We're going for poachers." And the trio set off for a nearby fishery.

PC Gary "Gazza" Wilson was a mountain of a man who had a scholarship from the School of Hard Knocks and a degree from the University of Life. As a time served plumber his exploits in a multitude of council properties had been of great benefit to him. Gazza was a good thief taker, with a quick wit and a keen mind. He was able to converse with anyone, be it the town centre yob, vagrant or member of the intelligentsia. Gazza had been chosen to take a fledgling rookie under his wing and on this occasion, his protégé was Mike Prince, one of a new breed of recruits with impressive academic qualifications and aspirations towards the higher echelons of the service. Sadly, he was rather short on common sense and his naivety demonstrated his lack of worldly experience. If Gazza was a rough diamond then Prince was fool's gold.

En route to the newly-stocked ten-acre lodge, the sergeant detailed his plan of attack. He discussed the offences involved ensuring that if arrests were made the young tyro would know what to do.

"Sergeant I have been looking at the Salmon and Freshwater Fisheries Act but I cannot find any definition of a fishery?" he pronounced, attempting to curry favour. The sergeant was impressed with Prince's knowledge of the poaching laws, but guessed that he had been well primed as poaching law was the sergeant's pet subject.

"Ah well lad, some questions cannot be answered by law books alone. A fishery is like a beautiful woman - impossible to describe but you will know one when you see one." Prince's eyeballs whirled in their orbits flummoxed by his sergeant's philosophical reply.

With engine and lights turned off the car freewheeled silently down the hill and parked on the verge. Closing the doors quietly, the poaching posse proceeded stealthily to a stile leading to the waterside. The lake was set in a beautiful valley dotted with copses and picturesque stone cottages. The far side was open and suited to fly fishing, but the bank they were to investigate was a poacher's paradise. The adjoining field sloped down to within ten feet of the water's edge and then dropped vertically in to heavy cover on the bank. The trees and bushes provided excellent camouflage for unofficial piscators and anchors for their set lines.

From their vantage point on the stile, they scanned the bank, in vain, for several minutes. Plan B was to check the bank for any telltale signs of poaching activity so they strolled across the meadow drinking in the fresh morning air to the call of the coot and the croaking heron. Sergeant Whyte was surprised at Gazza's noticeable apprehension as they approached a herd of gently grazing cows. He had always thought Gazza feared neither man nor beast, but it appeared he might have discovered Gazza's Achilles' heel.

"What's up Gazza? They are only cows!"

"What about that big bogger there? Are you sure it's not a bull?" he queried hesitantly.

"Bulls don't have teats Gary." mocked the sergeant. Realising that Gazza was not convinced, he plucked a discarded chestnut paling from the grass and handed it to the tremulous officer.

"Protect yourself from the nasty cows with that." He jibed.

Having circumvented the herd, Sergeant Whyte led them Indian file along the bank in search of forgotten lines. Prince bimbled along at the back, wondering whether this lake was a beautiful girl. Then, suddenly, there was movement in the distance as a figure darted into the bushes. Gazza and the sergeant ducked down hoping they had not been seen and waved frantically at the hapless Prince, hoping to switch him back on to reality.

At last, his attention was diverted to the job in hand and they ran along the bank to find three young men pulling in a superb specimen of salmo gairdnerii. They were so engrossed in landing the rainbow as to be completely oblivious to the police presence until Gazza's voice boomed out.

"Nar then me lads. That's a fine fish tharz got."

Three startled poachers jumped out of their skins and spun on their heels, perchance to flee, but froze in their tracks on seeing the officers silhouetted above against the rising sun. It must have been an awesome sight with Big Gazza towering over their heads, the intimidating thwack of chestnut against wellie echoing around the valley.

"Get up here! Face down! On the grass!" growled Gazza. The petrified poachers scrambled frantically to the top of the muddy slope and lay spread-eagled amongst the cowpats at Gazza's feet.

A quick check for weapons and they were restored to an upright posture, their apprehension relieved by a joke, a smile and the realisation that they would not be on the receiving end of a paling.

"Fetch the rest of them lines in." Ordered the sergeant and they slithered back to the water to retrieve their illegal instruments. Sergeant Whyte looked on in dismay as one heavy fish turned out to be a lowly inedible tench. His spirits were soon revived however, as the next line produced a fine rainbow.

"Shall I let this one go Sergeant?" queried the poacher. "Oh no lad! We need that for evidence." Commanded the Sergeant, thinking of his breakfast.

He then shuddered as the night angler took the fish in his left hand and crudely despatching it with several rabbit punches from his fist.

Fishermen and fishes were shipped off to the station, the former to be processed and bailed to court. The latter to be divided and devoured. It is amazing how the word gets round and a bantle of bobbies descended on the cell block anticipating a share of the spoils. Later that morning, even the Superintendent had the effrontery to enquire as to the whereabouts of his fish. He deserved one of course for his active role - being abed all night!

The now triumphant sergeant shared the catch with Gazza and Prince and, forgetting his ill-feeling over the lost frame, with his old snooker adversary. Urged on by his success, and the possibility of an invite to join the fishing syndicate, the sergeant and his anti-poaching squad, returned the next morning. This time the bank was unoccupied, but as they strolled along their attention was drawn to a threshing in the water. Several yards out at the end of a fallen tree trunk was a fish hooked on a set line and tangled around the end of a bough. For humanitarian reasons (the Sergeant's breakfast) the flailing fish had to be retrieved. How was this to be achieved? Several methods were proffered and discussed. If the mountain would not come to Mohammed then Mohammed must go to the mountain. But who was to be Mohammed? The day had begun to dawn, in more ways than one, on young Prince.

"l suppose I'm expected to do it." he offered, resigned to his fate.

"Better a volunteer than a pressed man." encouraged the sergeant.

Prince dropped his blue serge trousers, pulled on a pair of wellies and strode manfully to the edge of the watery mirror. Wisps of mist rose from the glassy surface. There he stood, blue shirttails hanging over his Y-fronts, his thin legs, white and goose-pimpled. After contemplating the wisdom of his decision Prince edged slowly along the trunk until the cold grey, waters lapped dangerously close to his manhood. Numerous encouraging sounds from the safety of the shore were followed by muffled sniggers and stifled laughter. Prince was recalled,

"l've got to give you credit lad. It was a good try." praised the sergeant. "We'll leave that one to the bailiff and his boat."

The Yokel and the Yuppie

It was a balmy summer evening in the secluded moorland hamlet of Maybrook. Ducks glided back and forth on the millpond, sheep grazed the close-cropped verges fronting the straggle of cottages, village post office-come-general store and the pub. Picnic benches, the types that combine a table and seat, outside the Dog and Duck were for the use of passing tourists and ramblers, but Old Tom, preferred the pew against the pub wall. From this vantage point, he could observe the gyrations of fellow patrons trying to park their bodies without spilling their ale. The pitch pine pew had been salvaged from the chapel in Bridgefield when it was converted into a des.res. 2 rcpts. 3 beds. Etc., for sale at umpteen thousand pounds. It had lost its former glory, the varnish now cracked and blistered by extremes of wind, rain and occasionally warm sun.

Tom relaxed in the evening glow sucking gently on the pipe hanging in the corner of his mouth. An occasional wisp of blue smoke navigated the contours of his flat tweed cap, set slightly askew over one ear. In his weather beaten, ruddy complexion could be observed - by those with the vision to see - a wealth of knowledge and experience. ln the close-knit rural community such commodities were valued and respected.

Tom had worked on the farm all his life. Starting as a lad, he had been part of the farming revolution. Although retired, Tom was neither redundant nor forgotten. He visited the farm daily for milk and eggs. He helped when they were short-handed, particularly at harvest time, and ferreted the odd rabbit for his favourite dish, rabbit and spar'rib pie. One of his greatest delights was to milk the beastings from a newly-calved cow for Annie to make one of her delicious custards. Fondest memories were of his shire horses, Belle and Bess, pulling the plough. He knew that tractors were more efficient but they were also noisy and reeked of diesel. Tom sipped at his mild and savoured the smell of horse and leather mingling with freshly turned earth, as his ladies leaned into their harness, the sun glinting on their muscle-rippled coats.

The sounding of a horn and the bleating of scurrying ewes interrupted Tom's reminiscences. Raising his eyes to the outskirts of the village, he saw a Japanese; short wheel-based, metallic yellow, go-faster-striped, four-wheel drive, pseudo Landrover. It was obviously a deluxe model, fitted with one of those matt black contraptions at the front for fending off a stampede of marauding shopping trolleys in Sainsbury's car park.

Headlamps blazing, the vehicle careered up the narrow road coming to a screeching and slithering halt outside the Dog and Duck. Tom eyed the fresh-faced young man, taking particular note of the check shirt and new blue wax cotton jacket. The driver looked up from his map scanning his surroundings.

"l say. You there!" he demanded in a brusque, well-tailored voice, as if hailing a city centre cab.

Tom, took offence at being compared to a black metal box on wheels, and responded with a bemused look.

"Duz tha mean me surr? He queried in a most servile manner. The young man's eyes searched all about Tom as if surveying an imaginary crowd and retorted sarcastically,

"Well I would hardly mean anybody else would I?"

Tom gave a shrug of his shoulders and raised his eyebrows in the way of an embarrassed child being admonished by teacher.

"Where the hell am I?" continued the young man.

"I suppose thar's frum city. Thar'll be one o'them kumputer progrummers or summat. Won't tha?" Tom observed.

"Yes I am actually." Responded the young man in a more agreeable tone. Realising the need to humour the old fool, he changed tack,

"Look can you tell me where I am. This map is hopeless." He pleaded.

Tom scratched the side of his head, readjusted his displaced cap, screwed up his face, and closed one eye as if in deep thought.

"Where's tha tryin' to git to surr?" he replied, a little more helpfully.

"Bridgefield. The old chapel that's for sale."

"Aah. Tha'll be lookin' furra kuntry 'ouse will tha'?"

"Yes. I am actually. A second home for holidays and weekends you know."

Tom's thoughts returned to his marriage in Bridgefield Chapel, the baptism of his sons and burial of his beloved Annie in the graveyard next to it.

"Well if I wurr goin' ter Bridgefill I wudna start frum ere surr."

The young man, tired and frustrated by his long journey, was in no mood to be the butt of some old yokel's jest.

"Is everybody round here as stupid as you?" he retorted angrily.

"Stupid I may be surr, but I'm not lost. Tha'll find Bridgefill darn that way - but I dunna know 'ow it'll find thee!" he instructed philosophically.

Shaking his head, he set off in an engine revving, clutch slipping, wheel spinning cloud of dust and gravel, leaving the ducks to settle once more on their pond. Tom managed a wry smile and downed the last of his mild, wiping the froth from his lips with the back of his hand. His blackthorn thumb stick tip-tapped on the stone flags of the ancient moorland footpath as he ambled away home muttering,

"Young'uns and townies - no respect for th'owd and kuntry."

An Evening with the Waltham Blacks

Gentle Reader, imagine if you will, it is the year of our Lord 1722. A wealthy tea merchant has attended to business over lunch in Thomas Garraway's coffee house in Exchange Alley, City of London. Garraway's was a venue for People of Quality and wealthy city traders. It was the first establishment to make the change from coffee to tea and served merchants directly engaged in the tea trade.

His ship had "come in" and in the early afternoon, he set off home on his mare, a pouch of gold coin hidden beneath his vestments and a short-barrelled "man-stopper" flintlock pistol in his pocket. His journey would take him out of the City and into a belt of rich sparsely populated farmland towards Waltham Forest.

The Royal Forest existed around the 13th Century, situated to north east of the City with the Forest of Essex on its northern boundary. Today, much of the land has been swallowed up by a new city of the same name, but in 1722, it was a vast wild tract of trees, laced with dark lanes and little or no habitation save an isolated dwelling or tavern. His home lay some miles off on the Essex side of the forest but he had trod this path before in safety.

As he and his mare entered the forest, the sun was starting to fall in the sky casting shadowy fingers around them and darkening the path ahead. As the sun dipped ever lower, the distant trees were silhouetted against the fading glow and a dark curtain was cast over the undercroft. Man and mare maintained a steady pace until the light ahead and behind was a pool of inky blackness. The sounds and sights of the night were all round, the hoot of an owl, the flight of a bat and the clip clop of his faithful mare.

They were well into the forest when the mare suddenly stumbled and came to a halt holding her front fore leg off the ground. A stone in her hoof rendered her lame and she may have slipped her shoulder. Our merchant dismounted to examine the hoof, reasoning that she could be ridden no further that night.

There had been much talk in those parts of gangs of rogues and vagabonds poaching the King's deer and other atrocities but for his part he thought the accounts were, fables or much exaggerated. However, experience, the mistress of fools, would teach him a lesson.

What a dilemma! Should he stumble on or limp back towards the City begging succour at a farmstead. He recalled a tavern deeper in the forest and chose to proceed. He was now vulnerable to any blaggard, footpad, robber or Highwayman who may happen upon him. He took comfort from the double-barrels of the pistol secreted in his coat pocket, checking that it was immediately to hand. His senses were tuned to every rattling pebble, creaking tree or snapping twig, the cough of a horse, call of a vixen or a human voice. Leading his horse onward, he stopped suddenly. What could he see in the distance? A light perhaps? Taking a few faltering steps he was sure it was a light, perhaps a candle in a window and his heart lifted and his pace quickened as a second light appeared.

Now he saw the outline of a building, a substantial one, two stories perchance a tavern where he could stable the mare and get a bed for the night. Arriving outside he was met by the landlord who received him very civilly, but on perceiving the horse was so lame as scarce to be able to stir a step, he grew uneasy. When asked about lodging for the night our weary traveller found there was no room at the inn. The lady of the house appeared, who told him most forcefully that he could not and indeed, should not stay there, wanting him on his way.

The merchant placed a crown in her hand with the promise of another for his lodging. Relenting she said there was indeed a little bed above stairs, on which she should order a clean pair of sheets to be put, for she was persuaded he was more of a gentleman than to take any notice of what he may witness there!

The merchant was uneasy fearing he was in a den of highwaymen, and expected nothing less than to be robbed and his throat cut. Was he a fly in a spider's web?

Having stabled the mare he settled in the bar. Suddenly the crackling of the fire was drowned by the sounds of three or four men alighting from their mounts in the stable yard. The landlord was quick to advise the men of his presence saying, "Indeed, brother, you need not be uneasy, I am positive the gentleman's a man of honour."

A voice exclaimed,

"Faith, I don't apprehend half the danger you do. I dare say the gentleman would be glad of our company, and we should be pleased with his. Come, hang fear, I'll lead the way."

Five men entered the bar, armed and all heavily disguised with blackened faces. Accosting the merchant with great civility, they invited him to honour them with his company to supper. His host was keen to explain their presence as "a gang of whimsical merry fellows, who are so mad as to run the greatest hazards for a haunch of venison or to spend a merry evening."

About ten o'clock there was a very great noise of horses, and soon after men's feet tramping the stairs to a room overhead. He could see the glimmer of candles through the gaps in the floorboards as the dust trickled down the rays of candlelight.

His host led him up the stairs to meet a man, more dignified than the rest, sitting at the end of the table, advising that he should not refuse to pay his respects to Prince Oroonoko, King of the Blacks!

Indeed, all present had blackened faces to compliment their disguises and their leader sat in front of a large stone fireplace above which hung the antlers of a sixteen point Monarch Red Deer. The merchant finally realised who those worthy persons were and in whose company he had accidentally fallen, but the fear he was in had clouded his judgement of the most evident signs.

Supper consisted of eighteen dishes of venison in every shape, roasted, boiled with broth, hashed collops [thin slices], pasties, umble pies [a pie filled with chopped or minced offal, and a large haunch in the middle, larded.

The long table filled the entire top floor and accommodated in all twenty-one persons. Each had a bottle of claret at his elbow, and the man and woman of the house sat down at the lower end. Two or three of the fellows had good natural voices, and so the evening was spent as merrily as the rakes might pass theirs in the King's Arms, or the City apprentices with their master's maids at Sadler's Wells.

During the course of their feast the traveller was beguiled with details of their rules and ceremonies. The Black Prince assured him that their government was perfectly monarchial, and that when upon expeditions he had an absolute command; "but in the time of peace", continued he, "and at the table, I condescend to eat and drink familiarly with my subjects as friends.

“We admit no man into our society until he has been twice drunk with us, that we may be perfectly acquainted with his temper, in compliance with the old proverb, ‘women, children and drunken folks speak truth.’ As soon as we have determined to admit him, he is then to equip himself with a good mare or gelding, a brace of pistols, and a gun of the size of this, to lie on the saddle-bow. Then he is sworn upon the horns over the chimney, and having a new name conferred by the society, is thereby entered upon the roll, and from that day forward, considered as a lawful member."

Around 2am, the revelry ended and our weary traveller slid in to the clean sheets on his bed but failed to sleep all night as he reflected on the evening’s events. He was unable to resolve with himself whether these humorous gentlemen in masquerade were to be ranked as knight-errants, or plain robbers since drinking was their delight, and plundering their employment. For you must know it is the first article in their creed that there is no sin in deer-stealing.

The merchant’s meeting with the Waltham Blacks is recorded in a letter to his friend and is the only known account of their meetings and initiations.

For many social and political reasons the Waltham Blacks and similar gangs were seen as a threat to the establishment. Running riot through the countryside they threatened, assaulted and even killed those who challenged or sought to prosecute them. Extortion, cattle-maiming, the firing of crops and buildings were common forms of retaliation. “Deer-stealing” may not have been a sin but raiding the King’s personal wine convoy was a heinous crime, even treason perhaps. Government feared these gangs were part of a national insurrection or revolution and something drastic had to be done.

There was nothing more drastic nor more penal than the Black Act of 1723 introducing the death penalty for over 350 offences, including being found disguised in a forest and carrying a weapon.

For good measure all the activities associated with the gang were also made felonies retrospectively, as all persons who had committed such offences were required to surrender, make a full confession and give names of all accomplices whereby a free pardon was granted. Suspects who refused to surrender within 40 days could be summarily judged guilty and sentenced to execution if they were apprehended. One element, totally alien to English law, was to render all inhabitants of a Hundred [local region] subject to a communal penalty, being punished if they failed to find, prosecute and convict alleged criminals. To ensure a goodly flow of intelligence informers were promised free pardons.

King's Messengers were sent to Berkshire to arrest the ringleaders but finding them in force chose to seek their cooperation as witnesses tricking them into going voluntarily to give evidence on the promise of being handsomely rewarded. The stratagem worked and forty Horse Grenadiers were despatched to round up the remaining gang members. Forty Blacks were tried at Reading Assize in 1723, four were hanged and thirty-six transported. It was considered that "those country rakes were constrained to vent their profligate dispositions in less dangerous employments."

That was the end of the Waltham Blacks, but not the Black Act, remaining in force until 1823. The judiciary were keen to enforce the most severe penalties of execution or transportation for the most minor infringements. However, they did occasionally exhibit some "leniency" as in the case of Tyrell and Adams whose wives pleaded at Stowe Court to have their husbands returned home. Lord Cobham promised their return within the week and seven days later a cart delivered two coffins to their door.

Its repeal heralded a new approach to the problems of crime and punishment but one side effect was the relegation of poaching offences to the bottom of the league in terms of penalties and enforcement.

The Wounded Poacher

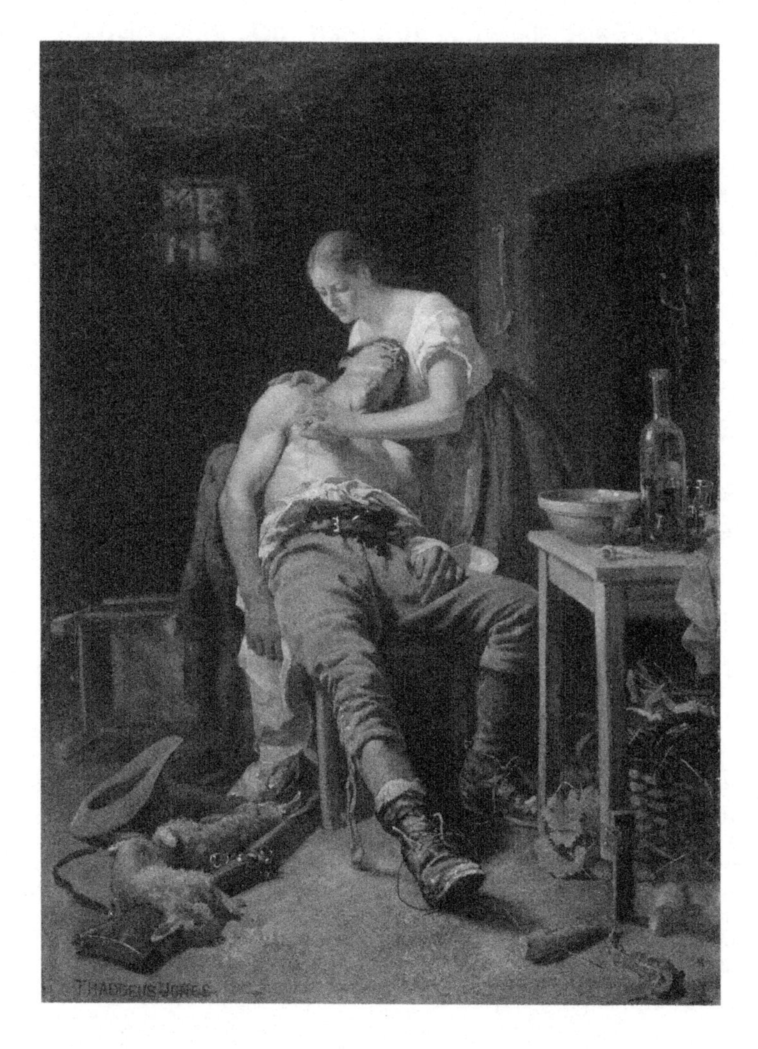

The Wounded Poacher Henry Jones Thaddeus (1859 – 1929)

The Black Act failed to put an end to poaching, being the pastime of nobility and clergy, and popular with Dragoons and Hussars and many soldiers returned from fighting in numerous conflicts. Keepers and poachers were often heavily armed with cudgel, cutlass or firearm. The hilt of a broken cutlass was recovered from a pond following one such encounter commemorated on a plaque at Langwith Lodge, Derbyshire.

"This sword was used by Chapman, the Captain of a Gang of fourteen Poachers, from Bolsover, who, with their faces blackened, and a white band on their left arm, attacked Col. Welfitt's Keepers, six in number, in Scarcliffe Park, on the 23rd November, 1850. One man, (a poacher), Rhodes, was shot dead; Chapman cut Thos. Booth on the back of the head, and severed a piece of the skull which was produced in Court at the Trial at Derby in the following Spring. The thirteen men were followed to Bolsover immediately by Col. Welfitt, at two o'clock in the morning, and all taken. They were tried at Derby, at the Assizes in March, 1851, when all were found Guilty. Chapman was sentenced to transportation for life, two for fifteen years, four for ten years, and the remainder for eighteen months' imprisonment.

The Sword was wanted on the Trial, but was not found until after, in a Pond in Bolsover, the broken piece in Scarcliffe Park, where the fight was, the following Spring."

S.W.WELFITT Langwith Lodge September 3rd 1867

The affray was the subject of a large wall mural in a public house in Bolsover for decades.

Such affrays or "poaching wars" were commonplace with injuries and deaths on both sides. Many estates had large establishments of gamekeepers engaged on night watching so poachers operated in strength. In one example, a poaching gang lured keepers into a wood, surrounded and held them captive at gunpoint while the poachers plundered.

Today incidents involving the criminal use of firearms against police and public are two-a-penny. The price of civilisation perhaps! It was not always so, as shown in the Derbyshire Police "Shooting Outrages on the Police" recording a single "outrage" in the years 1908 to 1912. On 27 December 1910 at Shirebrook, [next village to Langwith] five officers went to a house where 10 or 12 known poachers gathered to execute an arrest warrant on one of them under the Poaching Prevention Act. On gaining entry, they were quickly expelled and followed into the street by one of the gang who shot at them.

Why do poachers poach? There was a need for some to feed their poverty-stricken families and with the advent of the railways, game could be crated and sent to the London markets. This is most eloquently described in "I Walked by Night. Being The Life & History Of The King Of The Norfolk Poachers." Written by Fred Rolfe and edited by Lilias Rider Haggard. Fred writes in a phonetic spelling style so his written word can be confusing until one reads aloud, phonetically, and the true meaning becomes clear. Quite charming.

He was a lone poacher going about his business quietly without disturbing the keepers and crating his game for the morning train. Much of his book is a discourse on rural life, customs and society including some very strange cures and witchcraft.

For some, poaching would be a challenge to the social and political structure of haves and have not's and the philosophy that wild birds and animals were put on this earth for the benefit of all mankind, not just the powerful landowning establishment.

The painting of The Wounded Poacher brings to mind a story my father told me. He was a police officer and a farmer's wife pleaded with him to stop her husband from going poaching. She often found her husband early morning in the kitchen, the floor strewn with pheasants. At night, he would cycle from his home, not far from Langwith, into the adjoining counties to poach pheasants. He had no need for the game as he could shoot whatever he wanted on his farm. Perhaps it was a sport, a challenge, a test of his field craft. One night it was a poach too far and, meeting his match, he took a severe beating and our wounded poacher gave up the game.

One infamous Midlands gang of deer poachers gained quite a reputation. The Barnsley Deer Gang was not one single gang but a large group of small gangs operating in 4x4 vehicles over a wide area. Their own video shows their pickup bouncing across the fields after a Roe deer, its rear white end bobbing up and down under the lamp. Releasing dogs in hot pursuit, a broad Yorkshire accent shouts,

"Get another dog out! Get another fucking dog out!"

The excitement in his voice is intense and you feel the adrenalin, the buzz. The dogs soon bring the hapless deer to the ground where it is finished off with a hammer blow and a knife. "That's the way tha' fuckin duz it." is pronounced with a sense of great satisfaction and pride that leads me to believe that there is more to the sport, the pursuit or seeing a dog work than the financial gain. I have always held that for these reasons poaching can never be prevented.

Fred Rolfe records a detailed insight into the poverty of rural workers. At the age of twelve Fred served a month's hard labour with endless hours working the treadmill and picking oakum for killing a rabbit. In his case, the harsh lesson only determined him to follow the Game. Despite trying other jobs, including gamekeeping, he continued his illegal career with increasing relish. His book records the lives of many tough, fascinating characters struggling to survive in an era of rural hardship.

One night he was caught by four keepers and beaten within an inch of his life and taken to the lock-up. The next morning the police, fearing for his life, took him to King's Lynn hospital. He was arrested two weeks later as he left hospital and sentenced to twenty one days. Fred says,

"I was just as eager as ever. In fact I had got such a liking for the Game I was past stopping. Poaching is something like drug-taking, once begun no goen back, it get hold of you. The life of a poacher is any thing but a happy one, still it is exciting at times, and the excitement go a long way to soothe his conscience if it trouble him.

In the old days of sixty years ago [1870 perhaps] men were often driven to that kind of life by hard times. Since then some do it for the sake of sport, and the excitement of the game, that was so in my case, and a great many more beside, I loved the excitement of the job. Beside you had the satisfaction of knowing that you had the keepers and the police beat, and that went a long way towards recompense for the danger and risk run."

Fred must have been a considerable thorn in the keepers' flesh. In one example he drew a large net over a crop of roosting partridge taking 165 birds in one fell swoop the week before the start of the season. It was ever likely they would exact their revenge if they caught him.

Oh, 'tis my delight on a shining night, in the season of the year – a line from The Lincolnshire Poacher.

William the Conqueror's Forest Laws imposed frightening punitive measures on his new subjects. For rape, a man would lose the appendage with which he had disported himself! The "Tyranny of the Forest Laws" was equally savage where disturbing a deer could result in blinding or having a hand cut off. Killing a deer could lead to execution.

Neither were their dogs immune, if forest officials believed they could be used for illegal hunting. Dogs unable to pass through a lawing ring, a measuring hoop on a wooden block would have the middle two toes of their front paws amputated or 'expedited' to prevent them from chasing game. In The Poacher and the Squire by Charles Chevenix-Trench, he says that poachers are forever innovative and ingenious when evading the law and inhabitants of the New Forest trained pigs to point and retrieve. One such pig, named Slut, is pictured in Chevenix-Trench's book. Gentle reader, a word of warning! Do not search for the picture on Google if you are of a delicate disposition!

Sold for sixpence

For many years, poaching was a local affair where keepers lived cheek by jowl with poachers and knew each other well. It was common for poacher to taunt keeper when they met in the street or watering hole. One such occasion is described in Shots From a Lawyer's Gun by Nicholas Everitt.

A new keeper was at his wit's end trying to catch the poacher and his lurcher taking hares. The keeper's life and family were often threatened in a game of bluff. One Saturday evening the keeper came across the poacher accompanied by several equally choice blackguards and the infamous lurcher.

The keeper chose to chafe the poacher about the value of his dog and the poacher retaliated in a similar vein. Keeper enquired as to the dog's breeding and staying power and finally asked the price of the dog. Unwittingly the poacher replied,

"Well as you are such a pal of mine, and the dog would be of more service to you than anyone else, I'll say sixpence to you."

The keeper, quick as lightening says,

"Done wid ye at the proice." Snatching the gun from his shoulder, he shot the dog dead, tossing a sixpence to the poacher. Naturally, there were some fisticuffs.

The Game Act 1831 contained an unusual power whereby Lords of Manors could appoint gamekeepers authorised "to seize and take for the use of such lord or steward all such dogs, nets, and other engines and instruments for the killing or taking of game as shall be used by any person not authorised to kill game for want of a game certificate." This little known and seldom used power remained in force until 2007. There were tales of dogs being taken, or shot on sight but in modern times, it was thought to be rather inappropriate.

The introductory text to the Night Poaching Act 1828 states, "And whereas the Practice of going out by night for the purpose of destroying Game has very much increased of late years, and has in very many instances led to the commission of Murder, and of other grievous offences; and it is expedient to make more effectual Provisions than now by law exist for repressing such practice."

The Act created many new offences and although penalties were harsh they were not hanging offences. A first conviction was three months "and kept to hard labour" breaking stone, oakum picking and treading the treadmill. A third offence rendered the night poacher liable to transportation. The offer of violence to a keeper rendered the night miscreant liable to be transported for seven years, or imprisoned for two years. Three or more acting together with one armed was a more serious misdemeanour.

The prison treadmill was a common form of hard labour using manpower to crush corn or pump water.

The Game Act 1831 repealed laws created in the reigns of King Richard II, King Edward IV, Kings Henry VII and VIII. Daytime poaching was considered far less serious than night poaching as reflected in the penalty of a fine not exceeding £5.

Over the centuries, game, rabbits and venison were a staple part of the diet but in modern times and the advent of meat being plucked, drawn and wrapped in plastic its popularity has waned. In prosecutions, the value placed on a dead pheasant was often far less than that of a supermarket chicken. It was, and remains, common knowledge that a brace of pheasants can be purchased for a meagre sum from a shoot, but the birds do still come with their coats on and innards intact. Many are unwilling to pluck and draw as our grandparents might have done. Consequently, the value or importance of poaching diminished and was not high on police priorities. Apart from damage and disturbance a failure to prosecute could be taken as a sign of weakness leaving gamekeepers, their families and property further exposed to violence, intimidation and financial loss.

However, in 1991 the case of Haslam v CPS reflected the true value of a bird, fish or deer to an estate when Derby Crown Court awarded damages. Haslam was fined £45 for night poaching, £652 for firearms offences and £340 compensation at £10 per bird.

This ruling was the catalyst for restorative justice, especially on the trout rivers and fisheries of Derbyshire. What constitutes a fishery? I asked this question when writing Fair Game because in a plethora of English law there was no definition of a fishery. Could you condense all manner of waters, and how they might be administered by clubs, landowners and societies into one simple phrase? The answer is "A fishery is like a beautiful woman. You know one when you see one."

Poachers caught by river keepers have two options. Pay the going rate or face the police. The going rate was around £20 per fish based on the management costs, rent, wages, purchase of fish etc.

Confiscation of tackle was followed by a trip to the hole in the wall putting money back in the fishing club coffers.

The Poacher Drive

The ragged line of guns and beaters awaited the keeper's signal to start the hare drive around Boltby Park. The rolling hills of the estate, incorporating large areas of stubble, hedgerows and broad field margins, had proved to be excellent wildlife and game habitat. Even the keeper was called Pheasant.

The terrain also suited the brown hare but the once seasonal pursuit over the stubble by the poaching long dog men was now a year round problem. Traditionally hare numbers had been kept in check by a hare drive, also serving as a means of harvesting them.

The hare drive consisted of many walking guns lined out over a large expanse and walking slowly in encircling the hares. At the sound of Malcolm's whistle, the line snaked across the fields wheeling past several copses dotted across the landscape. Startled hares lolloped away in front. After several minutes, the line of guns rounded one such copse to find three local lads and their lurchers engaged in a bit of unofficial coursing. Surprised at the concentrated abundance of hares they had been oblivious to the approaching throng as they worked their dogs.

The sudden realisation that the hunters had become the hunted showed in their pale and anxious faces. Frozen like rabbits in a lamper's beam, they were unable to escape the pincer movement as forty or more men gradually encircled them. As the noose tightened, they awaited the coup de grace.

The beaters crowded round forming a menacing wall three or four deep. The uneasy silence was broken as Malcolm passed sentence.

"Right me lads. It's the police for you!"

Fetching the police, followed by a one-way ride to the nick, subsequent questioning, a long walk home and a court appearance, would only prolong their agony. It may have been for these reasons that a self-appointed spokesman pleaded on their behalf.

“Oh come on Mester Pheasant can't you just give us a good hiding and let us go."

His fellow poachers seemed perturbed at this suggestion but the option of summary justice no doubt appealed to some present, eagerly anticipating Malcolm's accession to their plea.

"Well we could give you a good hiding....." he paused rubbing his chin in thought, "....How many of us do you want to thump you?"

Spot Goes On Holiday

Old Tom had not been too well for some time and was in hospital for a few weeks. In the meantime, Spot went to stay with Tom's brother. After a few days in the new neighbourhood, Spot found a pub selling his favourite bitter and called in for a pint. Although taken aback by Spot's order the barman was quick to seize the opportunity for a fast buck.

"That'll be five pounds please. You know we don't get many dogs drinking in here."

"At five pounds a pint I'm not surprised!" retorted Spot.

Spot Goes To Crufts

Whilst many of us make the annual pilgrimage to the Game Fair, Spot prefers to visit the Crufts canine extravaganza. Although of rather mixed parentage Spot is proud of his working background and has no designs on being a pampered pooch, but he does enjoy casting an admiring eye over an array of upper-class pedigree talent and studying the latest fashions in doggy hairdos and designer accessories by Poochi.

Spot sat on the pavement as a stream of hopeful champions paraded before him. He noticed an obvious newcomer, a young Afghan called Prancing Cottonsox of Penge IV or Fred to his friends.

Fred stood uneasily in the queue. His freshly shampooed fur shielded from the elements by a protective coat, his tail and feet bandaged and head a mass of curlers. He felt rather conspicuous having seen his reflection in a shop window and was pleased to natter with Spot. Spot offered to let Fred in through a fire exit and bypass the queue. Fred declined the invitation but both agreed to see each other after the show.

The two dogs met, as arranged. The Afghan looked far happier, now regaled in rosettes. Spot appeared rather weary and bedraggled, as if he had been dragged through a hedge backwards. But he did have a twinkle in his eye.

"How did you get on then Fred?"

"Oh very well thank you. A first, two seconds and a highly recommended." Replied Fred enthusiastically. "What about you Spot?"

"A great day indeed Fred. I've had two bitches, four fights and I'm highly satisfied!"

Acknowledgement

Some of the stories are based on real events and some are complete fiction but many of the main characters are styled on friends and work colleagues who have provided encouragement and support in my police career and the pursuits of shooting and fishing. I hope my appreciation will overcome any possible embarrassment.

John Paley's artistic ability brings the stories to life with cartoons demonstrating that his knowledge of country sports and sense of humour made him the ideal illustrator for this book.

Rear cover photograph of author by Mark Sharratt.

The Wounded Poacher Henry Jones Thaddeus (1859 - 1929) Public Domain via Wikimedia Commons

Treadmill at Brixton Prison in London: British Library, Public domain, via Wikimedia Commons

Garroway's Coffee House George Walter Thornbury, Public Domain Wikimedia Commons

Books By This Author

Law Of The Countryside

A handbook for the Countryside Management Association

Fair Game – The Law Of Country Sports And The Protection Of Wildlife [Co-Author John Thornley Obe]

A comprehensive guide for the layman to the law relating to country sports and conservation and protection of wildlife.

Shaggy Dog Stories - 1996

Sixteen short stories about country life and sport, plus Spot the beer-drinking, domino-playing shaggy dog, who pops up throughout the book to prove that man is a dog's best friend.

Deer: Law And Liabilities [Co-Author John Thornley Obe] - 2000

The law and liabilities relating to deer in the U.K.

The Hidden Glen Carla Parkes

It's Fresher's Week at Portsmouth University and Emma is thrown into the melting pot that independent life and university bring. She befriends three girls from different backgrounds and levels in society. Perhaps these innocents abroad are attracted to each other by their common denominator – being insular, not worldly wise, not streetwise, but together they would look to each other and after each other in a lasting friendship.

Explore Emma's childhood, her "Uni" friends, the men in her life, her sailing and rambling adventures from Scotland to the south coast, France, Italy and the Peak District.

Through difficult, emotional times, she is guided by the wisdom of her wonderfully philosophical "Nannee Jane" who always finds positive outcomes on her encounters, rather like Jane Austen. Is there a link between Nannee Jane and Jane Austen apart from family connections with Chawton?

Following several false starts and one disturbing end to a relationship, Emma continues her quest to find her perfect man. Hoping to find peace and solitude away from nine-to-five in a London fashion house, she embarks on a lone, wild-walking, trek in the Scottish Highlands where she meets a mysterious fellow traveller in a remote fishing hut. The events that follow in the Hidden Glen remain unfathomable, magical, mystical and beyond all human reasoning.

Emma returns to her family and university friends where she reveals almost all her secrets. Several years later Emma retraces her steps, but this time she is not alone, in a quest to find the man, love and the happiness she left behind in the Hidden Glen. Discover whether her quest results in a happy reunion with her man of mystery. Emma seeks to unravel some of the mysteries of the glen and the lovers' potential return to reality. Will her quest result in a happy reunion with her man of mystery? The text is illuminated with Jane Austen quotations about love, marriage and happiness as relevant now as the day she wrote them.

Lavishly illustrated with photographs so you can walk in Emma's footsteps or even visit all the locations except, that is, for the Hidden Glen.

Printed in Great Britain
by Amazon

23670411R00079